# M

## BEST SE

A chance to read and collect some of the best-loved novels from Mills & Boon—the world's largest publisher of romantic fiction.

Every month, four titles by favourite Mills & Boon authors will be re-published in the *Best Seller Romance* series.

A list of other titles in the *Best Seller Romance* series can be found at the end of this book.

Helen Bianchin

# THE
# HILLS OF HOME

**MILLS & BOON LIMITED**
LONDON · TORONTO

*First published 1977*
*Australian copyright 1978*
*Philippine copyright 1978*
*This edition 1984*

© Helen Bianchin 1977

ISBN 0 263 74700 X

*Set in Linotype Baskerville 11 on 11½ pt.*
*02–0584*
*Made and printed in Great Britain by*
*Richard Clay (The Chaucer Press) Ltd,*
*Bungay, Suffolk*

# CHAPTER ONE

'SHELLEY! Am I early, or are you late?'

'A bit of both,' Shelley answered pensively, viewing her blonde sleep-tousled flatmate over the brim of her cup. 'Coffee?'

'Please,' Inga begged as she slipped down into a chair opposite. 'Oh, how I hate Mondays,' she declared, attempting to stifle a prodigious yawn. 'Such a day should be abolished, or declared a compensatory malaise!'

'One of those weekends?' Shelley enquired teasingly, and her smoky-blue eyes sparkled with laughter as Inga made an exaggerated moue.

'Hardly—I was presented for parental approval, remember?'

'Dare I ask how things went—or is the subject taboo?' Shelley questioned lightly.

'Out of a possible ten points, I might have gained one,' Inga imparted with wry wit as she sipped her coffee. 'To be earning my living as a model is bad enough, but to be Swedish as well ...' she trailed off wickedly. 'I was almost tempted to adopt a heavy accent in self-defence and plead a language problem!'

'Didn't you tell them that you were Australian-born?'

Inga wrinkled her nose expressively. 'It wouldn't have made much difference. Bart's mama is a for-

5

midable matron whose Victorian principles make me wonder how she ever managed to conceive a son. One gathers the impression it was engineered by remote control.'

'Exit the eminently eligible Bart,' Shelley concluded with a slight smile.

'Well, Mama controls the purse-strings,' Inga alleged impudently. 'How was your weekend?'

Shelley made a non-committal gesture with one hand. 'So-so.'

'Incredibly dull, in other words.'

'Not really,' Shelley replied easily. 'Adrienne gave one of her impromptu parties——'

'—which you obligingly spent all day Saturday catering for,' Inga uttered knowingly. 'And cleaned up afterwards, I'll be bound. Without doubt Adrienne conveniently developed one of her headaches?'

'A day down at Surfer's Paradise, actually,' Shelley informed her with a grin, and Inga gave an indescribable snort by way of reply.

'Any worthwhile men in attendance at the party?'

'That depends on how you define "worthwhile",' Shelley declared wryly.

'I know what you mean,' the other girl grimaced. 'At the witching hour of midnight the charming debonair male you've been pleasantly conversing with all evening suddenly decides there's no time to be lost and begins steering you towards the bedroom. If you happen to be unwilling, you're abandoned quicker than you can bat an eyelash.'

'Invariably!'

'Speaking of charming males, isn't it about time that gorgeous stepbrother of yours put in an appearance?'

'The cane season is well under way,' Shelley replied slowly. 'He'll be fairly busy harvesting.'

'Now there's a man who could transport me into a state of blissful Nirvana,' Inga vouchsafed enviously, and Shelley smiled lopsidedly as she felt a familiar clutch at her heartstrings.

'He does seem to have that effect,' she managed with a light laugh, and suffered Inga's speculative glance.

'Well, he does have several attributes in his favour,' Inga declared candidly. 'Besides being ruggedly good-looking, he's eligible and terribly rich. He attracts women like bees round a honey-pot. Strange he hasn't married,' she pondered thoughtfully. 'He's over thirty, surely?'

'Thirty-three,' Shelley replied abstractedly, unable to dismiss Mitch's raw-boned features from her mind. Tall and indomitable, his skin deeply tanned from hours in a tropical sun that had streaked his light-brown hair to a tawny-gold.

'It's eight-thirty, Shelley,' Inga reminded her, breaking in on her reverie. 'You'd better get moving if you're to catch that bus.'

Shelley quickly stood to her feet, collected a capacious leather shoulder-bag from its resting place against the table-leg, and flung a hurried—' 'Bye, see you tonight'—over her shoulder as she sped out the door.

At the end of the driveway she glimpsed the bus lumbering to a halt to allow a passenger to alight, and only an energetic sprint saved her from missing it entirely.

By the time she had regained her breath the bus was cruising at a moderate speed along the main north road. At this comparatively early hour the heavier flow of traffic was surging in the opposite

7

direction towards the city. Shelley gazed idly out at the familiar suburban houses with their neat lawns and gardens blooming in the early spring. The school where she taught a new entrants' class was less than a mile away and she invariably elected to walk the distance, but this morning she'd woken with a premonition that today wasn't going to run its usual course, and wondering why she had slowed her actions to a point where she was unusually late in leaving the flat.

It had been that song again, a Denver/Danoff composition that always succeeded in bringing a lump to her throat, sending her thoughts winging homeward, and this morning hadn't been an exception.

Unconsciously a slightly wistful sigh escaped her lips. Home was several miles north of Mossman, in Queensland—a sprawling white-painted wooden homestead nestling against the foothills, looking out over acre upon acre of gently-swaying green-leafed sugarcane.

Her mind winged back to the day Luke Ballantyne had swept her widowed mother into marriage. In Brisbane on business, he had taken one look at Cathie Anderson behind her office desk and promptly invited her to lunch. Scarcely aware of doing so, Cathie agreed, and three days later Luke proposed, successfully quashing every argument she presented. That Cathie had an eleven-year-old daughter hadn't discouraged him in the least. He was that kind of man—open-hearted, warm, and generous by nature. Shelley had *belonged* from the onset.

In musing reflection, Shelley thought of the gauche, overawed young girl she had then been—so ready to embrace her new father, his home, all his possessions. How impossibly earnest she must have seemed, longing for a complete family as the realisation of her girlish dreams.

Luke and Cathie had shared a love that radiated an aura all of its own, and for Shelley there was Luke's son. Mitchell Ballantyne—tall, broad-framed, rough-hewn, and twelve years her senior. He accepted Cathie with a warmth that was genuine, and tolerated Shelley with an indolent charm. Under his teasing tuition, she'd learnt to drive the gleaming sedan as well as the Range-Rover. She attended a boarding-school in Herberton on the Atherton Tableland, several miles distant, from which she returned during mid-term breaks and at the end of each term. After boarding-school had come a year at university, followed by teaching college in Brisbane, and each time she travelled home she was wont to wonder how she could ever tear herself away from the lovely homestead and its surrounding acres.

Ballantyne and sugarcane were synonymous, and as there were cattle barons, so were there cane barons—among whom Luke Ballantyne ranked as one of the wealthiest in the North Queensland sugar belt. It seemed ironical that after years of having to watch every cent, Cathie was to enjoy less than five years of financial security as Luke's wife. Tragedy struck in the form of a rare blood disease, for which there was no available cure.

The sound of children's excited voices interrupted Shelley's thoughts, bringing the present sharply into focus, and one glance at her surroundings confirmed that the bus had drawn to a halt outside the school's main entrance.

'Aren't you coming, Miss Anderson?'

Shelley turned, smiling as she recognised the cheerful freckle-faced young girl standing beside her seat. 'Thanks for reminding me, Cindy. I was miles away,' she offered in explanation, moving quickly out into the aisle.

'I guess you were thinking,' the youngster declared as they stepped down on to the footpath.

'You're right—I was,' she agreed absently.

'There's Amanda waiting for me. 'Bye, Miss Anderson.' With a wave Cindy began to run, and Shelley was left to follow at a more sedate pace.

The irregular group of school buildings glowed in the morning sunlight, setting several panes of glass agleam and sparkling. She felt an affection for this place, her first post as a fully-fledged teacher, and wondered if she'd continue to feel the same in years to come.

The walk across the playground to her classroom brought forth greetings from several young children who stopped mid-play to bid her welcome. She enjoyed the experience of teaching, possessing a natural flair with the young. 'Chalk in your veins', Mitch had often commented teasingly, and such reflection brought a winsome smile to her lips.

The morning progressed much as usual, and immediately after lunch she began sorting out coloured cut-outs she used to demonstrate rudimentary mathematics, surveying her young pupils with indulgence. A story, followed by thirty minutes of singing, should be adequate compensation for time spent on mathematics, which at this level was not a favoured subject.

Some twenty minutes later Shelley's explanation was abruptly interrupted by a knock at the door and entrance into the classroom of a fellow staff member.

'I'll take over, Shelley. Miss Pattison wants to see you in her office.'

Shelley's eyebrow rose in silent query, and was met with a slight shake of the head by way of reply.

'The only clue I can offer—the Head's fighting to retain a composure that's obviously been ruffled, and as neither woman nor children can manage to achieve that state, it has to be a man,' Cybil Jardine inferred cynically.

'Surely not an irate parent?' Shelley hazarded quickly. 'It's usually the mother who visits junior school,' she intimated with a faint frown before turning back to meet the children's interested curiosity. A brief explanation ensued, together with a stern admonition to behave while Mrs Jardine took the class during her absence.

As she stepped briskly along the corridor Shelley puzzled over the sudden summons, for she could recollect no misdemeanour of which she might be guilty. Whatever it was, it must be important, otherwise the Head would not have permitted an interruption in the middle of class.

'Come in.'

Shelley stifled a brief surge of anxiety and obeyed the muted command, shutting the door quietly behind her before turning to face the illustrious Miss Pattison.

Her eyes widened with incredulity as she glimpsed the tall powerful figure standing near a window on the far side of the room.

Mitch! Attired in dark tan trousers, an equally dark dynamic masculinity.

'Miss Anderson.'

Shelley quickly swung her startled gaze back to the woman behind the large desk. Miss Pattison, headmistress and stern disciplinarian, was affectionately referred to as 'Patty-dragon' by staff and pupils alike.

'Mr Ballantyne wishes to speak with you on a matter of some importance,' Miss Pattison said brusquely, and for a brief second the semblance of a smile seemed to lighten her heavy features. 'I can only sanction his proposal and accede to his wishes —reluctantly, I must add,' she evinced dryly as she rose to her feet. 'You may have the use of my office,' she voiced courteously to the large-framed man standing so thoroughly at ease several feet away before turning back to face Shelley. 'Goodbye, my dear.'

Miss Pattison met Shelley's startled gaze with a slight twinkle—hitherto rarely glimpsed—then patted Shelley's arm before moving briskly across the room and out through the door.

'Whatever is Patty-dragon talking about?' Shelley swung frank curious smoky-blue eyes round to meet the musing gleam evident in Mitch's dark tawny gaze.

'Is that what you call her? Apt,' he declared succinctly.

'Mitchell Ballantyne! Will you please explain what you're doing here?'

'It's invariably "Mitchell" when you're vexed,' he mused lazily. 'But not often do I get the added affixation of Ballantyne.'

With a gesture that betrayed impatience she tugged the edge of her denim jacket and smoothed an imaginary crease in her skirt. 'I'm employed

12

here to teach,' she uttered crossly, 'and right now I have a class to get back to!'

'Wrong,' Mitch corrected mildly as he moved forward with lithe ease. 'We're both leaving this establishment within the next ten minutes. In less than two hours we'll board a plain to Cairns.' He lifted an idle hand and smoothed a stray tendril of long ash-blonde hair back behind her ear, then tilted her chin. 'Luke has a heart disorder. It's inoperable, and the medical professionals predict that he has less than a month.' His expression softened as he saw the genuine distress mirrored in her eyes. 'He wants you home, Shelley. Is that too much to ask?'

'Of course not,' she voiced shakily. 'I'd do anything for Luke.'

'I'd counted on that,' Mitch acknowledged quietly. 'Your Patty-dragon took some persuading. However, a donation to her favourite cause clinched matters, and you can rest assured you're quite free to leave, as of now.'

'The library fund,' Shelley deduced knowingly. 'You made a sizeable contribution—without doubt!'

His smile was faintly cynical. 'Quite.'

She met those lazy tawny eyes of his and was unable to read much from their expression. A hand lifted itself almost of its own volition and smoothed down the length of her hair. It was a purely nervous gesture, and doubtless didn't fool him in the slightest. He was all too aware of the effect he had on her—darn him! For however seemingly indolent, those dark golden eyes never missed a trick, and not only did he possess the knack of being able to read her mind, he was invariably one jump ahead —which to say the least of it was disconcerting.

'I suppose I'm expected to bid my pupils fare-well, pack my belongings, and leave the flat in reasonable order—all in the space of an hour, or less?' she queried with resignation.

'Something like that.'

The amused indulgence in his tone made her cross. 'Why didn't you telephone yesterday, or even last night?'

'It was easier to present you with a *fait accompli*,' he drawled mockingly. 'With due respect, little one, you're no match against Patty-dragon.' He reached out and lightly grasped her elbow, urging her to-wards the door. 'There's little time to waste if we're to make that plane. I'll wait in the car while you say your farewells. Don't be long,' he commanded firmly.

'Five minutes,' she promised as she followed him out into the entrance foyer.

It wasn't easy making excuses to the children, and there was no time to offer an explanation to Cybil Jardine.

'I'll write just as soon as I can,' she promised as she took her leave from the classroom, and stepping along the corridor she couldn't help the slight sigh that escaped her lips. Heaven knows when she'd be back within these walls. At the moment she wasn't willing to hazard the number of weeks she'd need to be away.

From the main entrance Shelley slipped quickly down the steps towards the car, and the engine started up as she drew close. Mitch leaned sideways to unclasp the door, and as soon as she was safely seated he put the car into gear.

'I suppose the Ballantyne protective instinct is responsible for me not knowing anything about

Luke's illness?' Shelley questioned almost as soon as he had eased the sedan out from the school grounds.

The glance Mitch spared her was calm and penetrating. 'I detect a note of censure there, little one. It was Luke's decision to keep you in ignorance, not mine.'

She watched in idle fascination as his large sun-weathered hands swung the wheel hard to the left, then let it spin back as the car straightened out into the steady stream of traffic. Broad-framed and rugged, he emanated a sense of deliberate calm—an almost lazy indolence that was misleading, for he frequently achieved twice as much as any one of his workers in a like amount of time. Nothing seemed an effort, yet he could move with the swiftness of a tiger, and with equal deadliness. Only once had she witnessed his anger, and she still blanched as the memory of that occasion came to mind.

A young eighteen and home on vacation, she had returned from a party at an hour much later than her permitted curfew. Barely a year since Cathie's death, Luke had been away down south on business. Feeling exceedingly guilty, she had crept indoors and was almost to her room when Mitch emerged into the hall from the study. His silence was more eloquent than mere words could ever have been. When her jumbled explanation finally came to a halt, he had reached out, drawn her close against him, then kissed her with a devastating thoroughness. 'I won't answer for the consequences if ever you put me through these last few hours again.' Brusque, incredibly bleak words that offered no apology.

For days afterwards she had viewed him with a wariness that merely brought forth a glimmer of amusement, and for the first time ever she looked forward to leaving the homestead and returning south to teaching college.

Ballantyne hospitality being what it was, there was never any difficulty in inviting a friend to stay for the holidays, and there were numerous girls eager to ingratiate themselves for the sole purpose of angling such an invitation. Mitchell Ballantyne was considered a prize in the matrimonial stakes, and Shelley had swiftly become slightly cynical over the apparent friendship of all but a few of her fellow female students. However, the inherent honesty in her character compelled her to admit that while they made use of her in this manner, she was just as guilty by using their company as a shield against Mitch.

'Luke won't thank you for assuming an expression of melancholy,' Mitch's voice broke in on her thoughts. 'I'd advise you to begin practising that captivating smile of yours. At its brightest, it can lift lagging spirits sky-high.'

Shelley swung smoky-blue eyes round to study his profile. 'How would you know?' she queried lightly. 'I doubt there's ever been a time when your spirits have lagged.'

'My, my,' he drawled with lazy mockery. 'What were you thinking about?'

'All the things I must do in the short time you've allowed me,' she prevaricated with seeming innocence, noticing that they were almost at her flat. 'Take the next street to the left.'

His lips twitched slightly. 'At least credit me with a reliable memory, young Shelley. Although not exactly a regular visitor, I have endeavoured to call whenever within cooee of this fair city.'

'Yes, I know,' she chuckled, and couldn't resist adding, 'I've never quite fathomed out whether it's to check up on me, or my two flatmates.'

'Both,' he slanted teasingly as he brought the car to a halt at the kerb. With lithe ease he slid from behind the wheel and snapped shut the door, sparing a quick glance at his watch as Shelley stepped out on to the footpath. 'This isn't the time for verbal one-upmanship, little one—save it to amuse me with on the plane. We've work to do.'

Shelley raised her eyes heavenward as his hand at her elbow forced her to move briskly towards the front flat.

'We?' she queried with wry scepticism. 'Your idea of packing is definitely the antithesis of mine!'

'Undoubtedly. However, as you're going home and not embarking on an ocean cruise, I fail to see that an impeccably-packed suitcase is essential. You have a choice—empty contents of drawers on to the bed for me to pack, or vice versa.'

'Vice versa, thank you,' she answered promptly over one shoulder as she unlocked the door.

'I suspect you're mindful of your own blushes, rather than mine,' he evinced dryly.

'I doubt you've ever blushed, Mitchell Ballantyne—even during your vulnerable teenage years.' She pulled a face at him. 'Everything you do is conducted with superb ease.'

'There's a few things you haven't caught up with yet,' Mitch slanted mockingly as he followed her inside.

The flat was just as she'd left it, and while not untidy, it bore a well-lived-in air. Numerous books lay scattered on chairs in the lounge, atop the dining-room table, and there was evidence of hastily discarded breakfast dishes reposing in the kitchen sink.

'I'll have to let the girls know I'll be away for a while,' Shelley began, and a slight frown creased her brow.

'No involved telephone conversations—there's not enough time. I chartered a Cessna from Cairns early this morning, and the pilot is standing by for a two-thirty take-off. Get to it, young Shelley,' Mitch bade decisively, reaching into the inside pocket of his suede jacket. 'Will a hundred dollars cover your share of sundry expenses?'

'For heaven's sake!' she expostulated, shooting him an angry glare. 'I do have money of my own.'

Ignoring her brief outburst, he queried with calm implacability, 'How much, Shelley?'

Oh, why did he always have to have the upper hand where she was concerned! 'It depends on how long I'll be away,' she allowed carefully with no intention of relenting.

Mitch regarded her solemnly for all of ten seconds, then said evenly, 'You won't be coming back.'

Shelley cast desperate eyes away from him and resorted to exasperation. 'Of course I'll be coming back. How can I not come back?'

He reached out a hand and tilted her chin, looking down into those smoky-blue eyes for a few timeless seconds before releasing her. 'Easily. Now, be a good girl and simply do as I tell you, hmm?'

'I can't just walk out,' she asserted heatedly. 'The girls will need to get someone else to share, and when I return I'll have to look for another flat. They're not easy to find,' she finished with slight resentment.

Silence resounded around the room until she

thought he must surely hear the rhythm of her breathing.

'We have exactly forty minutes in which to board that plane, and whether we do it with all of your belongings intact is entirely up to you,' he essayed with dangerous solemnity. 'I'll deal with arguments and explanations later, but not now.'

'You're a bully, do you know that?' she flung angrily.

'And you're behaving like one of your intractable young pupils,' he returned evenly, adding, 'in need of a sound slap or two.'

'I'm scarcely a spankable child!' Shelley was goaded into sallying resentfully.

'There are more subtle forms of punishment,' he returned wryly.

'Such as?'

Without a word he moved, and his swiftness caught her unawares. The hands that grasped her shoulders halted any attempt to struggle, and as his head descended she made one last desperate effort to escape that sensuous mouth, only to give a painful gasp as his hand tangled in the thickness of her hair.

His kiss began as a total invasion of her senses, and while it was in no way a brutal assault, it was nonetheless shattering and left her feeling treacherously weak-limbed and breathless.

'If you must play with fire, don't expect not to get burned,' he warned cryptically, letting his hands drop slowly to his sides.

'I hate you!' The cry came from deep within and almost choked her.

Mitch smiled sardonically, and for the briefest second there was a flicker of amusement in the depths of those dark amber eyes. 'You don't, but

19

that's something we'll sort out later.' Then, as he caught the suspicious shimmer in her eyes, he lifted a hand and touched her cheek with a gentle finger. 'Don't go all female on me, Shelley,' he bade softly. His lips touched hers fleetingly, lifted, settled again in a gentle caress, then releasing her, he straightened and moved round the table. 'Business, little one. How much is needed to square your share of expenses?'

'The rent is my responsibility, Mitch,' she protested shakily, making an all-out effort to regain her composure.

'Your independence from anything Ballantyne-gifted—*Mitchell* Ballantyne-gifted,' he corrected wryly, 'is that important?'

'You don't understand.' It didn't help that she understood even less.

He seemed about to say something, then changed his mind. 'Have it your way, little one,' he accorded enigmatically.

Fifteen minutes later the bulk of her packing was completed, although hardly in an orderly fashion, as Mitch had simply pulled out two drawers and tipped their entire contents on to the bed, then filled each suitcase to capacity with clothes of every description. He appeared not a whit embarrassed by an array of wispy undergarments, and she couldn't help pondering over his apparent familiarity with such things.

There was little time for anything but a brief assessment of her share of the rent before scrawling her name across the bottom of a cheque and attaching it to the crucially short note that Mitch had penned in explanation.

They reached the airport and relinquished the

hired car, skirting the main building as he led her towards a side entrance, then on to the tarmac where the Cessna stood waiting. It wasn't until they were airborne that Shelley had the opportunity to ask and get answers to her questions regarding Luke's state of health.

'Theoretically, he should be in hospital,' Mitch indicated dryly. 'However, with infamous Ballantyne tenacity, he flatly refuses to go—on the grounds that the hospital can't do anything more for him than the ministrations of a registered nurse in his own home. He argues that although he can't predict *when*, he intends determining the *where* of it.' He shrugged negligibly and extracted cigarettes and a lighter from his jacket pocket. 'I'm inclined to agree with him.' The lighter flared, and he paused fractionally before expelling the smoke with evident satisfaction. 'The doctor calls every few days, and it was he who arranged for a nurse to live in.'

Shelley glanced at him curiously. 'What is she like?'

'Typical feminine curiosity, young Shelley?' Mitch shot her a slow smile. 'Emma Stone is a paragon of efficiency. Young—mid-twenties, I'd say. Other than that, I'll leave you to form your own opinion.'

His voice was carefully bland, she determined wryly. Impossible to tell whether the nurse was a friendly soul or a competent martinet.

'I imagine Luke has to rest most of the time,' she broached pensively, and caught his slight nod of agreement.

'He assents to an afternoon siesta, and retires early to bed.'

Shelley shifted her gaze outside the small window

to the great expanse of sky, feeling indescribably sad. Luke wasn't old, barely sixty, and had always seemed to maintain good health. However, it couldn't have been so at all, for heart conditions didn't just happen, they developed gradually over a period of years.

'I should warn you that Louise has declared her intention to descend within the next few days.'

Mitch's deep drawl intruded upon her thoughts and brought a slight grimace to her lips.

'Oh dear,' was all she could think of to say right then.

' "Oh dear" is right,' he echoed sardonically.

Louise Cartwright was Luke's sister, and about as similar in nature to her brother as chalk was to cheese. A veritable pillar of a Sydney suburban community, she adored managing everything from church fêtes to charity affairs, and manipulating people was her forte.

'Is——' Shelley stopped herself from saying 'that man' just in time, '——Hal coming?'

'I've no doubt he'll leap at the opportunity,' Mitch evinced cynically. 'It will present an ideal argument to escape the necessary bonds of labour. He bothers you?'

The query was so swift and unexpected that it left her floundering for words. 'Not—really. How— what do you mean?'

'You know precisely what I mean, Shelley,' he stated dryly. 'Louise imagines his roving eye stops at visual appreciation, but I happen to know otherwise. No prevarication this time, little one.' His voice was suddenly hard and dangerous.

Troubled smoky-blue eyes met those of tawny gold. 'Most of what he says is subtle *double en-*

*tendre*,' she offered slowly. 'Louise seems to find it amusing. It's difficult to explain—other than that I feel uncomfortable in his company,' she finished unhappily.

'Hmm,' Mitch commented noncommittally.

It was something of a relief when the Cessna began its descent to refuel at Townville, and after a brief stopover they flew on to Cairns.

The air was noticeably warmer, despite that it was late afternoon and not yet summer, and Shelley felt the customary sense of expectancy that always seemed to greet her each time her feet touched down on the tarmac here. For it meant she was almost home, barely an hour's drive away, and unconsciously her lips parted in a contented smile.

In no time at all Mitch stowed her suitcase into the boot of his large Chrysler sedan, and was soon heading the car out towards the main road.

Shelley's first glimpse of cane on the outskirts of the city brought a surge of well-being to her veins. Tall and lush green, swaying softly in the warm air, it was a welcome sight. Soon, narrow steel tracks began to cross and re-cross the bitumen road, linking each farm to the main rail line leading to the mill.

It had to be the tropical climate of the Far North that was responsible for the azure sky, creating the red-brown soil to contrast sharply with the green of growing cane. The ribbon of bitumen curved gently inland for several miles before swinging back towards the coastline at Ellis Beach where aged coconut-palm trees spread their leafy fronds above tussock grass and sparkling white sand. The sea looked cool and inviting, translucent depth merging from green to blue.

She sat in contented silence as Mitch eased the car

23

around numerous bends as the road hugged the foot-hills that rose from the rocky foreshore. Before long they would leave the coast behind, and once past Port Douglas they would be less than twenty minutes' drive from home.

Unbidden, the words of John Denver's composition lilted silently inside her head, and never had they seemed more appropriate than they did right now. 'Country road, take me home, to the place I belong'. Pure nostalgia, she sighed serenely.

Suddenly her expression sobered, and the silent words trailed to a halt as she realised that this could well be the last time she would be able to call it home. After Luke's death the homestead she loved so dearly and its surrounding acres would belong to Mitch. To visit, even occasionally, would tear her apart, for she wouldn't be able to bear seeing the woman Mitch would ultimately select as his wife presiding in that beloved homestead. And there would be children—Mitch would want a son to inherit the vast acreage of Ballantyne cane and the not inconsiderable wealth that was part of it all.

A pain began beneath her ribs and rapidly became a physical ache. Somehow, she had to get through these next few weeks without becoming an emotional wreck. Time enough to give in to heart-break when she was back in Brisbane and alone. She would write, of course, and eventually Mitch would pass her carefully-written letters to his wife to answer. Then, after a time when their invitations were consistently, albeit politely, refused, the correspondence would dwindle down to the customary card each Christmas.

It all flashed before her eyes in a matter of seconds, and she caught a glimpse of herself ten years from now—a restless, characterless creature unable to accept second-best, with a reputation among her pupils for being a dragony martinet. God forbid she should ever become a replica of Patty-dragon!

'Come back from wherever you've been, young Shelley. We're almost there.'

The soft teasing drawl brought her thoughts back to the present with a jolt, and she forced a smile to her lips, safe in the knowledge that he would never know the effort it cost.

'Yes,' she agreed quietly. 'Not long now.'

In only a matter of minutes the car would slow and turn down the road leading to the homestead settling on the first gentle slopes of the hills rising to form part of the Great Dividing Range that ran from Cape York in the north all the way down into New South Wales.

She even managed to hold the smile in place during the sharp perceptive glance Mitch spared her, and by the time he brought the vehicle to a halt beneath the spreading branches of a mango tree near the side entrance of the house, she was relatively composed.

Luke had supervised its construction over twenty years ago. A large sprawling dwelling, simply designed, its numerous rooms led off from a wide centre hall. There were six bedrooms in all, two bathrooms, a spacious lounge, a study, a large dining-room and an even larger kitchen. French doors opened from each room on to a wide screened verandah that ran around the entire house.

'Home, Shelley,' Mitch announced steadily. 'This time, to stay.'

At once her composure was shattered, and she turned bewildered eyes to meet his, the silent question in their depths unable to find a voice.

'There's absolutely no doubt about it,' he drawled enigmatically, then touched her arm and drew attention to the sprightly figure stepping quickly down towards them from the verandah. 'Here's Janet.'

## CHAPTER TWO

'You've arrived safely,' Janet greeted with fond enthusiasm as they slid out from the car.

Shelley's face creased into a wide smile. 'Janet, it's good to see you again.' She moved round the front of the car and hugged the well-rounded figure affectionately. Janet Atkinson had been with the Ballantyne family since the death of Luke's first wife, twenty-three years ago, and was very much part of the household.

'It's time you were home where you belong,' came the swift rejoinder, to be quickly followed by a barely-concealed sniff, hastily disguised, and there was a brightness in Janet's eyes that Shelley couldn't help but regard with suspicion.

'Hey!' she laughed chidingly. 'It's barely three months since I was last here.' Her expression sobered, and she moved back a step. 'How's Luke?'

'Impatiently waiting, I daresay,' Mitch broke in laconically as he hefted suitcases out from the boot of the car.

With an arm round Janet's waist, Shelley walked

the short distance to the house, giving in to temptation as she allowed her gaze to wander lovingly over the great sprawling building and nearby gardens, the trees and the shrubs.

If ever there was a living memory of her mother, it was here in this garden. After years of flat-dwelling, Cathie had at last been able to indulge her green fingers by developing a flower garden and shrubbery, and under her gentle care a riot of colour began to abound. In spring there were the bauhinias, pale pink and faintly striped with red, and in summer the delicate pink and cream frangipanni exuded a sweet-smelling fragrance. Then there was the jacaranda, the gardenias and camellias, the large clusters of tubular-shaped flowers of the stephanotis and the purple bougainvillea.

'I know I must vie with the garden for your attention, but now it's my turn.'

At the sound of that deep quizzical drawl, Shelley's head quickly swung back to the house and the lean-framed man in a wheelchair gliding slowly along the verandah towards the top of the steps.

'Luke!' His name came from her throat as a light bubbly sound, and without further thought she ran up the steps straight into the curve of his outstretched arm.

'Ah, young Shelley,' Luke murmured softly as she untangled herself to stand close beside him, clasping a large tanned hand in her own.

'I didn't get anything like that by way of a greeting.' This from Mitch, with a twinkle in his tawny eyes. 'Even Janet commanded a display of affection that was sadly lacking in the welcome I received.'

Shelley tilted her chin and regarded him musingly, slipping easily into the light teasing banter

27

they exchanged without rancour. It was only when she was alone with him that she felt way out of her depth.

'Sorry, Mitch,' she twinkled unrepentantly. 'Patty-dragon and her office effected a somewhat dampening influence.'

'I'll hold you to that belated welcome at a more appropriate time,' he slanted blandly, although his eyes held a wicked gleam.

Shelley shifted her sparkling gaze back to Luke and uttered an eloquent sigh. 'One of these days I'll manage to have the last word,' she declared ruefully.

'Not a chance, little one.' Mitch smiled, then cast his attention to the slight figure hovering in the doorway. 'Emma, come and be introduced,' he bade informally as the nurse came forward to join them. 'Emma Stone—Shelley.'

Shelley smiled and murmured a friendly greeting, aware of the other girl's swift appraisal.

'I've heard a lot about you,' Emma indicated politely, adding—'From Mr Ballantyne senior, of course.'

Shelley didn't dare spare a glance in Mitch's direction for fear she'd burst into laughter. Good heavens, surely Emma didn't accord him the appellation of *junior*!

'I'm almost afraid to ask whether I've been flattered or flattened,' she quipped lightly, and looked down at Luke with mock-despair. 'What have you been saying?'

'Oh, this and that,' he condescended tolerantly.

'I expect you'll want to freshen up before dinner,' Janet intervened amiably.

'Give me thirty minutes, then I'll come and help you in the kitchen,' she smiled happily, and there

28

was an answering warmth in Janet's smile.

Shelley allowed the affection evident in her smoky-blue eyes to swing back to the man at her side. 'You've acquired a sophisticated mode of tranportation since I was last home,' she indicated teasingly.

'Battery-controlled,' Luke grinned. 'Had it sent up from Sydney.'

Her expression sobered and she gently squeezed his hand. 'You deserve to be spoilt.'

'Be assured that he is,' Mitch chuckled deeply as he bent his lengthy frame to grasp a suitcase in each hand. 'I'll put these in your room.'

After Mitch disappeared down the hall, Luke gave a sigh of satisfaction and looked long into the face of the young girl beside him.

'It's good to have you home, Shelley,' he said simply.

Tears sprang unbidden to her eyes and she blinked rapidly. 'It's good to be here.' This would never do. Home barely five minutes, and already she was beginning to come apart. Mitch was right in warning that Luke would be averse to any emotional display. 'Hey,' she managed shakily, 'aren't you going to show me what this wheelchair can do?'

'Walk beside me, and I'll put it through its paces.' A touch on the control panel and the chair began to move silently towards a ramp covering the single step from the verandah into the house.

Once inside, Luke directed it down the hall to a smooth halt outside her bedroom door. 'Managed that corner pretty well, wouldn't you say?' he chuckled lightly, then tilted his head to one side to look up at her. 'Aren't you going to give praise for my efforts?'

29

'Definitely deserves an "A",' she twinkled gaily, and leaning down bestowed a fleeting kiss to his brow. 'I've half an hour in which to shower and unpack before dinner. See you soon.'

Unpacking was achieved with the utmost simplicity—it was merely a matter of separating what needed to be ironed, which seemed to be almost everything, owing to Mitch's preference for speed versus neatness, and relegating the remaining articles in drawers.

It was almost six o'clock when Shelley crossed the hall and made her way towards the kitchen. A knee-length denim skirt topped with a fashionable short-sleeved body shirt of matching blue looked fresh and neat, and her ash-blonde hair had been released from its chignon to swing loosely about her shoulders. Slightly less than medium height, she was slim with soft curves in all the right places, nicely-shaped legs, and a clear honey-clear skin. A wide mobile mouth, an inconspicuous nose set beneath widely-spaced sparkling smoky-blue eyes completed an appearance that was infinitely attractive.

An appetising aroma wafted from the large modern kitchen, and Shelley allowed her eyes to wander over its sparkling appliances with affection. The hub of the house, this was her favourite room, for here she could indulge her culinary skills to her heart's content and thus give Janet a welcome respite.

'Your timing is perfect,' Janet welcomed appreciatively.

Shelley smiled as she moved across the mosaic-patterned vinyl floor to stand by the wall-oven. 'Chicken,' she deduced lightly. 'As only you can prepare it. My digestive juices are positively flowing in anticipation!'

'Flatterer!' came the chuckling reply.

Shelley cast a quick glance towards the adjoining dining-room, then moved across to the large dutch dresser. 'I'll set the table.'

'Don't set a place for Luke,' Janet intimated as she swiftly drained saucepans of their contents. 'His wheelchair has a specially-fitted tray that clips on.' Adroitly changing the subject, she queried with genuine concern, 'There were no problems at the school?'

Shelley shot her an amused look as she placed cutlery on to the large rectangular-shaped table. 'Can you imagine anything deterring Mitch from his objective?'

Janet began to laugh. 'Quite frankly, no.'

'He'll meet his match one day,' Shelley declared positively, and missed Janet's quick discerning glance.

'Perhaps he already has,' the older woman stated thoughtfully.

'Oh?' Carefully casual, Shelley valiantly tried to ignore the way her stomach lurched sickeningly. 'Who is it this time?'

'Carry these serving dishes to the table, Shelley,' Janet instructed briskly, and whisking off her apron took a dish in each hand and followed suit. 'Go and tell them it's ready, there's a dear.'

Shelley shot her a puzzled look and met the other's bland smile. When Janet chose to retain information it was virtually impossible to prise anything from her—a veritable clam, in other words! No doubt she'd have to wait until Mitch chose to reveal details himself. Drat this jealousy of hers where he

31

was concerned—it wasn't fair to her nervous system!

She took a deep breath as she stepped through the doorway into the lounge. It was a spacious room, quite the largest in the house, and bore a well-lived-in air. Comfortable armchairs were strategically placed, and she caught the sound of Mitch's deep drawl followed by light feminine laughter.

'Janet advises dinner is ready,' Shelley managed with contrived cheerfulness as she moved into the room.

Luke looked up, gave her a singularly sweet smile, then held out a hand which she grasped unhesitatingly.

'I don't suppose I can deviate from that diet you insist upon?' He made it sound more like a statement than a query, and grimaced wryly when Emma swiftly shook her head. 'Consommé, lean steak and salad every night is not my idea of a satisfying meal,' he declared.

'Now, Mr Ballantyne,' Emma chided in a no-nonsense voice. 'A light diet is essential.'

Shelley's glance skimmed quickly from Luke's irritated expression across to the nurse. 'Surely that could be varied?' she felt compelled to enquire.

'Are you a dietitian?' There was subtle sarcasm in the query, and the look Emma cast her was far from friendly.

'Shelley's a darn good cook,' Luke defended warmly.

'Whatever her domestic capabilities, it's unlikely she has the specialised knowledge required to compile a diet programme for your specific heart disorder,' Emma rationalised with a light smile. She cast brown eyes gleaming with self-righteousness towards Mitch. 'You understand how important it is, don't you?'

'We all do, Emma,' Mitch replied appeasingly. 'I suspect my father's grumblings are merely an attempt to beget Shelley's sympathy.' Completely relaxed, he smiled at both girls and taking each by the arm he moved towards the door. 'Shall we go in to dinner?'

It was an excellent meal, for Janet had surpassed herself, and Shelley felt a pang of regret for Luke's plain fare by comparison. Conversation seemed to flow unceasingly, for the evening meal was regarded as an opportunity to discuss various interests as well as to catch up with local news, and therefore it was quite usual for them all to sit at the table for over an hour.

The work load of the cane farmer was seasonal, but even during the off-season there was always something requiring attention. The Ballantyne acreage of cane was large, its farm machinery extensive and expensive, and regular maintenance was a necessity. During the harvesting, mid-June to mid-November, Luke and Mitch rose before sun-up and were fully occupied until late afternoon, then in the evening often had to supervise the burning-off of cane to be cut the following day. A certain amount of paperwork was involved, with accounts and wages for the workers, as well as numerous investments that were Ballantyne-controlled. Shelley reflected idly that such responsibility must now rest solely on Mitch's broad shoulders.

She glanced around the table and encountered Emma's speculative brown eyes studying her unobtrusively, and couldn't help but feel vaguely irritated by the other girl's manner. That Emma had set her sights on Mitch was becoming increasingly obvious—a deduction Shelley assured herself had nothing to do with her own remarkable sensitivity where Mitch was concerned!

'How long has Emma been here?' she asked curiously of Janet as she stood in the kitchen drying dishes.

'Almost three weeks, to the day.'

'Heavens, you make it sound as if you've been counting them,' she murmured wryly.

Janet spared her a telling glance that spoke volumes. 'She's an excellent nurse. Let's leave it at that.'

'In other words, I wasn't imagining things,' she slanted sardonically.

'No,' came the succinct reply. 'Fortunately, Mitch is no fool.'

Shelley hung the damp cloth over the oven door, then quirked an enquiring eyebrow at Janet. 'Shall we join them?'

'Definitely,' the older woman chuckled in assent, tucking her arm through Shelley's as they left the kitchen.

Their joint entrance into the lounge brought a twinkle of humour to Mitch's tawny eyes.

'There you are,' Luke expressed affectionately. 'Come over here, young Shelley, and amuse me with some anecdotes about those pupils of yours.'

She couldn't help but smile as she crossed the room to his side. 'Things have been more hectic than usual, with the addition of a real "Dennis the menace" into the class,' she recounted lightly, and as his wheelchair was some distance from the nearest chair, she knelt down to sit comfortably at his feet.

'A terror, eh?' Luke chuckled.

'If you can count placing Herman, the school's pet carpet snake, into one of the girls' satchels the first day he arrived, and a frog into the drawer of my desk the following day,' she essayed with an impish grin, 'I think you'll get the general picture!'

'Horrible,' Emma grimaced distastefully. 'What did you do?'

'Suggested he bring another frog to keep the one he'd given me company,' she answered lightly.

'And did he?'

Shelley looked up at the sound of Mitch's amused drawl, and her eyes brimmed with laughter. 'Oh, yes. Several. All turning up in the most awkward places.'

'I'd have paddled his backside,' Janet asserted with a decided twinkle.

Shelley sobered quickly. 'I think he'd already had more than his share of that kind of discipline, poor mite.'

'I suppose you made him stand in a corner to contemplate the error of his ways,' Emma stated flatly, looking faintly bored.

Shelley shook her head. 'It took a few weeks before we reached an understanding.'

'How did you achieve that?'

Stone by name and stone by nature, Shelley perceived silently. 'By persuading him that he'd have far more of my attention if he concentrated on his lessons, instead of inventing childish pranks,' she related evenly.

Emma contrived a condescending smile. 'Your sister seems to favour a psychological approach,' she observed to Mitch with amusement.

'Shelley and I are not related,' he informed her easily. 'We don't even share a parent.'

'But Mr Ballantyne has often referred to her as his daughter,' the girl protested with a sudden rush.

'To me, Shelley *is* my daughter,' Luke stressed distinctly, and his expression softened as he looked down at the slight figure curled near his chair. 'Will you play for me?'

Shelley turned her head and met his smiling gaze with a singularly sweet smile of her own. 'Yes.'

Luke transferred his gaze to his son. 'You did say it had arrived?'

Mitch affirmed with a silent nod, and Shelley looked from one to the other with curiosity.

'An early birthday present,' Luke explained gently as Mitch left the room to return seconds later with a new guitar case.

'Open it,' Luke commanded, his eyes indulgent as they witnessed her delight.

She touched the clasp and gently lifted the lid with a feeling of awe for the instrument inside. 'It's beautiful—just beautiful!' she whispered, completely overwhelmed. A Spanish guitar was so expensive that only successful professionals could afford to acquire one. The knowledge that it would have had to be specially ordered brought tears to her eyes.

'Thank you,' she said simply, and impulsively caught Luke's hand and carried it to her lips.

'Ah, child,' he sighed gently. 'You're so like your mother.' There was a slight catch in his voice. 'Try the guitar.'

She took it from its case and held it reverently, lightly stroking the strings to find them perfectly tuned. Her hair fell forward to form a partially-concealing curtain from her small audience, and as she played she became oblivious to everything but the music.

Luke favoured country music, and the chords flowed easily beneath her fingers. The words inevitably found voice, and she sang unselfconsciously in a soft, melodically-true tone that was with one with the instrument. Unaware of an attempt to entertain, she drifted from one song to another, never faltering.

When she came to the end of the particularly poignant Denver composition 'Follow Me', a silence greeted her that remained unbroken for all of thirty seconds. In that time everything fell back into place as she became aware of the room and the people in it. A little nervously she turned and placed the guitar into its case and fastened the clasp, then pushed back her hair with fingers that shook slightly.

'Beautiful,' Luke commended softly.

She still felt a little bemused and knew it was evident. 'I'm sorry—I didn't realise the time,' she managed shakily.

'There's no need to apologise, little one.'

Shelley cast large darkened eyes slowly up to where Mitch was standing only a few feet away, and took the hand he held out to assist her to her feet.

'You really are quite talented, Shelley,' Emma commented in a patronising tone, and doubtless would have added something to that had it not been for the sound of a car on the driveway.

'It's almost eight-thirty,' Janet declared with a slight frown.

'Not too late for visiting,' Luke essayed blandly as Mitch crossed the room and disappeared towards the front door.

Within minutes he returned with a startlingly attractive girl at his side.

'Shelley, Mitch said you'd be coming back with him,' the girl exclaimed, her vivacious features alive, and Shelley responded with friendly warmth.

'Nice to see you, Belinda.'

'Sorry to intrude on your first night home, but I'm flying down south tomorrow and there were a few books Mitch had lent me that I wanted to return.'

Belinda Bellamy was the daughter of the local Shire councillor, and in spite of being an indulged only child she was totally unspoilt. Shelley reflected that in recent years since Belinda's mother's death she had accompanied her father on his various business trips, and acted as his hostess at numerous social functions.

'Where are you off to this time?' she enquired with interest.

'This trip is solely for my own benefit,' Belinda revealed engagingly. 'I need some time to sort things out, and what better than a three-week cruise around the Islands?'

'What indeed?' Mitch echoed with equanimity.

'Stay and have supper,' Janet bade kindly. 'Shelley was entertaining us. Perhaps she'll play some more.'

'Do, Shelley. Wow, is that a new acquisition?' Belinda queried as her eyes fell to the guitar case Shelley held.

'Luke's birthday gift,' Shelley affirmed, opening the case for inspection.

'That's really something. It's your twenty-first soon, isn't it? The key to the door and all that jazz?' Belinda queried laughingly, and Mitch slanted Shelley a devilish smile.

'She's had that for some time. However, I imagine we'll come up with something appropriate to celebrate the occasion.'

'You look scarcely more than eighteen,' Emma contributed grudgingly, causing Mitch to laugh.

'She's petite,' Luke alluded gently.

'All of two inches over five feet,' Mitch enlightened teasingly, and Shelley pulled a face at him.

'Two and a half inches, I'll have you know,' she retaliated. 'I've a good mind to hunt out my school uniform and plait my hair!'

'Play the guitar instead,' Belinda urged blithely. 'Don't take any notice of Mitch.'

'Oh, but I don't,' Shelley replied sweetly, casting a singularly wicked smile in his direction. 'He thinks an extra twelve inches and twelve years' difference gives him an edge.'

'Doesn't it?' he quizzed with lazy mockery, and Shelley grinned unrepentantly.

'I shan't answer that.'

'I'm keeping score, little one,' he divulged softly, and there was an elusive hint of steel beneath that quiet drawl. For a moment he held her gaze, then as an inexplicable shiver feathered down her spine she moved away and lowered herself to kneel close by Luke's chair, fingering the strings of her guitar.

'Lovely,' Luke commended gently some ten minutes later when she put the instrument to one side, and as she felt his hand on her shoulder she turned and gave him a smile.

'It's a beautiful instrument,' she accorded, only to have him shake his head.

'Wood, and steel strings—inanimate. Beneath your touch they come alive.'

39

Shelley felt her throat constrict at his compliment and couldn't utter a single word.

'Coffee, anyone?' Janet intervened briskly, and Belinda rose from the chair she occupied with an apologetic refusal.

'I really must go, there are still things I have to do,' she declined regretfully.

'I'll have mine later,' Emma declared as she spared a glance at her wristwatch before claiming Mitch's attention. 'If I could enlist your help, I'll get Mr Ballantyne ready for bed.'

'Come and talk to me for a while, Shelley,' Luke bade, and as she acquiesced willingly, Emma began to shake her head to the contrary.

'Mr Ballantyne has had quite enough excitement for one day. Time enough tomorrow for a cosy little chat.'

Dear heaven, she took the natural spontaneity out of everything! Cosy little chat, indeed! Shelley wondered how Mitch could present such a calm exterior, and extend that lazy charm of his to someone so lacking in sensitivity!

'In the morning,' she promised Luke gently as she leant down and touched her lips to his temple. 'Sleep well.'

'Goodnight, Luke,' Belinda extended a hand and touched his shoulder, her smile a trifle sad.

'Have a pleasant trip,' he encouraged kindly. 'Shelley will see you out.'

'He seems in very good spirits,' Belinda remarked as she slipped in behind the wheel of her car.

'Luke's a remarkable man,' Shelley vouchsafed gently. 'It must take considerable courage to maintain such an affable exterior.'

'It's a Ballantyne characteristic, that imperturbable shield,' Belinda answered wryly. 'I've known Mitch all my life and I've yet to scratch beneath its surface.'

It was on the tip of her tongue to make a laughing rebuttal, but the words died in her throat as she glimpsed the wistful expression on the other girl's face. Not Belinda too, she choked silently, wondering why the discovery should startle her when it was an ill-concealed fact that Mitch had only to beckon for any number of girls to come running—why not Belinda!

'Enjoy yourself on that cruise,' she managed lightly. 'If I weren't needed here, I might be tempted to join you.'

'Next time,' Belinda declared. 'Meantime, take care.' She switched on the engine and put the car into gear, then gave a nonchalant wave.

Janet was setting cups and saucers on to a tray when Shelley entered the kitchen, and the thought of sharing coffee and conversation with Mitch in Emma's presence made her feel indescribably weary. Emma could have him all to herself!

'I'm in need of an early night, Janet,' she pleaded. 'You don't mind, do you?'

'Of course not, child,' came the kind reply. 'Off you go and enjoy a good night's rest. Don't get up early—I intend spoiling you with a pre-breakfast cup of coffee in bed.'

Shelley gave her a quick hug. 'Did anyone tell you that you're an angel?'

'Oh, some!' Janet twinkled lightly.

Collecting her guitar case from the lounge, Shelley paused in the kitchen doorway and blew Janet a kiss before crossing the hall. In her bedroom, she placed the instrument gently on the floor

41

near the wall by her bed, and stifled a wide yawn. It was barely nine-thirty, but it felt hours later than that.

She must have fallen asleep almost as soon as her head touched the pillow, but now she was awake and unsure as to the reason why. As her eyes became accustomed to the darkness she checked her watch for the time, sure that dawn was not far distant, only to find it was barely a few minutes past midnight. For a moment she lay listening to the silence, and then she heard it. A soft whine, and a scratching against the verandah screen door.

Bessie! Without thought, Shelley scrambled out of bed, drew a brunchcoat on over her nightgown and sped barefoot out on to the verandah.

'Shh, girl! Steady now,' she whispered softly as she unlatched the screen door. An excited whimper of delight greeted her, followed by an animal welcome second to none! Bessie alternately rolled and bounded round in circles, all the time whimpering with ecstatic delight.

'She's taken to keeping odd hours of late,' Mitch's voice came quietly from somewhere behind.

Shelley straightened and turned to face him, her expressive features mirroring surprise that he was still dressed. 'You haven't been to bed yet,' she couldn't help stating with concern. 'Is Luke——?'

'Asleep hours ago,' he intervened steadily. 'I was in the study when Bessie decided she wanted in.'

'I hope she hasn't disturbed anyone.'

'Doubtful, young Shelley,' Mitch assured her solemnly, reaching into his shirt pocket for cigarettes and matches. 'Sit, Bessie.' It was a command that had immediate effect, for Bessie sat instantly and didn't move.

'I wish she'd do that for me,' Shelley declared rue-fully.

'She knows you're a pushover, and trades on it,' he intimated dryly.

She watched in idle fascination as he placed a cigarette between his lips, then struck a match and lifted it to his mouth between cupped hands. His eyes gleamed momentarily in the bright flare of light, and she shivered involuntarily. Why, oh, why did she always feel on edge with him, tongue-tied and unsure of herself?

'Luke seems happy enough,' she offered ten-tatively in an attempt to break the silence.

'Yes—now that you're home,' he agreed. His broad frame seemed to loom incredibly large in the thin thread of moonlight.

'How long has he had to use a wheelchair?'

'Since a stroke left him partially paralysed almost a month ago. If you notice, he uses only his right arm.'

She felt stricken, and raised sad eyes to meet his. 'It's——'

'Life,' Mitch pronounced quietly.

'Then life's unfair,' she cried bitterly, hating him for stripping it down to harsh reality.

'Constantly.'

'You're hard,' Shelley flung helplessly.

'Realistic, little one.'

'Oh, stop it!' she implored wretchedly.

'All this nervous pent-up emotion isn't going to alter anything, Shelley.' There was a gentleness in his voice that almost proved her undoing.

'I don't know how you can be so calm,' she said unhappily.

'Appearances can be deceptive.'

She immediately felt contrite. What a thoughtless idiot she was! 'I'm sorry.'

It seemed ages before he spoke. 'It's been a long day. Go back to bed, Shelley. I've a few things to check before turning in.'

Anxious to make amends, she queried heedlessly, 'Would you like me to make you some coffee?'

'If the making of it will help you sleep easier.'

She could sense the smile in his voice, and said irrelevantly, 'I haven't thanked you for smoothing the way with Patty-dragon.'

'So, thank me.'

'Now you're amused,' she declared with an expressive sigh.

'Come and make that coffee,' he advised quizzically. 'Otherwise I might insist that you deliver that belated welcome.'

'It's not that important, is it?' she queried as she fell into step beside him.

'The welcome, or the coffee?' he mocked tolerantly.

'I pity the woman who marries you, Mitchell Ballantyne,' she said severely. 'You'll lead her a terrible dance.'

'You think so?'

'Yes,' Shelley declared emphatically. 'She'll never know when to take you seriously.'

'She'll know,' Mitch drawled softly. 'I'll make sure of it.'

Yes, she thought dully, he would—in a manner that could leave no room for doubt.

The kitchen sprang to light as Mitch pressed the wall-switch, and in an instant Shelley brought her thoughts to a halt. Flashing him a bright smile, she turned and crossed to the servery-bench, glad to

44

have her hands occupied with the task of spooning ground coffee beans into the percolator.

'Emma seems to be dedicated to her profession,' she observed tentatively in the need to make conversation. 'Does Luke need attention through the night?'

'Rarely. A mild sedative ensures a relaxing sleep, and I always check him before turning in.'

Shelley took down a cup and saucer, then rummaged in the cake-tins for something to eat. 'Does Emma have any time off?' she queried curiously. 'Aren't there certain rules governing maximum duty hours per day, likewise the number of consecutive days without a break?'

'All taken care of,' Mitch's voice drawled from behind. 'Emma works weekdays, and a relieving nurse from the local hospital takes over at the weekend.'

The percolator seemed to be taking an age to heat, and she was all too aware of his disturbing presence a short distance away. Without consciously doing so she began to fidget with the sugar spoon.

'Sit down, Shelley,' he instructed enigmatically. 'You're agitating unnecessarily.'

'I am not,' she tossed angrily, nervously tucking a stray tendril of hair back behind her ear. 'Luke's welfare means a great deal to me.'

'I know it,' he assured her mildly, and began spooning sugar into his cup as soon as she set it down on the table. 'There's something I want to discuss with you.' His eyes caught and captured hers, and one glimpse at that intent unwavering gaze of his was enough to set the butterflies inside her stomach fluttering madly.

'I—it's late, Mitch,' she said quickly, casting her

45

eyes in the vicinity of his left shoulder—anywhere but directly at him. 'It can wait until tomorrow.' She touched shaky fingers at each temple. 'I have a slight headache.'

'You're lousy at fabrications, Shelley,' he evinced sardonically.

'If it's——' she began resentfully, then took a deep breath and started afresh. 'Janet implied——'

'Exactly what did Janet imply?'

'That you'd already met your match,' she said slowly. 'I suppose you'll be getting married before long. Is it Gianna?'

'Why should you imagine it might be Gianna Parelli?' he questioned thoughtfully.

'Perhaps it's Belinda, or the very beautiful Margot,' she sallied peevishly. 'I never could keep count of them all.'

'Have there been so many?' Now there was amusement in his voice.

'The link that holds me here will be severed when Luke dies—you know it, and so do I,' she was goaded into vexed speech.

'Wrong, Shelley.'

Blind anger prevailed. Her eyes flashed indignantly and her lips trembled with distress. 'I've loved every minute of the time I've spent here. But I'd be a fool if I thought it would always be my home.' Tears clouded her vision, and she swung away impatiently, intent on getting as far away from the enigmatic man seated at the table close by.

She was brought to a sudden halt by a large strong hand as it shot out and gripped her arm, and even as she struggled Mitch pinned her arms helplessly to her sides with an ease that was mortifying.

'Am I interrupting something?'

Shelley drew a shaky breath as Mitch released his grip. Heaven knew what would have happened if Emma hadn't chosen that precise moment to enter the kitchen. His eyes had been alive and dangerous, not carefully inscrutable or alight and lazily twinkling with humour. It didn't bear thinking about.

'Nothing that can't be continued later,' Mitch returned grimly.

Shelley seized the opportunity to escape, and hardly daring to look at him she murmured a cursory 'goodnight' that was meant to include Emma and all but ran from the room.

The sight of dear old Bessie lying curled up on the floor at the foot of her bed was the last proverbial straw, and with an inarticulate sound she slipped down on to her knees to hug the dog affectionately as hot tears slid ignominiously down her cheeks.

## CHAPTER THREE

'JANET!' Shelley exclaimed remorsefully as she scrambled to sit upright against the pillow. 'You shouldn't have let me sleep in.'

'Get away with you, child,' Janet chided gently as she placed a tray beside the bed. 'It's not that late.'

Shelley glanced at her wristwatch and wrinkled her nose expressively. 'When the rest of the household rises at six and breakfasts at seven—eight-thirty is late!'

'Rest easy, Shelley. Knowing you, I don't imagine you'll make a habit of it.'

Shelley grinned amiably and reached for her coffee. 'Any plans for today?'

The older woman sighed a little and sat down on the edge of the bed. 'You'll have heard that Louise intends spending some time with Luke?'

'Yes,' Shelley answered pensively, and nibbled at a piece of toast.

'Mitch took the call after you'd gone to bed. Louise, together with Hal and Lyn fly in tomorrow.'

'That means another trip to Cairns,' Shelley voiced slowly. 'Perhaps I could save Mitch the drive, and go down myself to meet them.'

Janet shook her head thoughtfully. 'I believe he intends relegating that duty to Ken.'

Ken Pemberton had been a permanent employee for the past twenty years, and Shelley liked him. He was slow-talking and rarely volunteered much by way of conversation, but he was a hard-working loyal man. Painfully shy, he insisted on being self-sufficient, and lived in a small cottage several hundred yards from the homestead. He cooked his own meals, maintained a vegetable garden, several hens and chickens, and seemed content with the company of his dog—a faithful spaniel-cross who bore the name 'Mutt'. Occasionally he could be persuaded to come up to the homestead on the pretext of partaking beer with Luke and Mitch in the early evening, but more often than not he chose to be alone. Shelley was his golden-haired angel, and they shared a rapport that was quite touching. Janet had tried unsuccessfully over the years to present him with various baking spoils, and offered unfailingly each year to undertake his spring-cleaning, but he

48

always refused. Without complaint he had accepted Shelley's cakes and biscuits in those early years when she baked more failures than successes, and she had only to hint at a need to spring-clean for him to suggest that she work off her energies on wiping down paintwork. He loved to whittle wood, and most of his spare time was spent creating beautiful figurines, several of which Shelley had in her possession, Christmas and birthday gifts over the past ten years.

'I don't suppose you'll refuse my help in the kitchen?' Shelley chuckled lightly, returning from her reflection as she recollected Louise's predilection for cakes and pastries together with numerous cups of tea throughout the day. 'I can see Emma's frowns with remarkable clarity, and predict at least one dinner-time lecture on the merits of a healthy staple diet,' she concluded dryly.

'Very probably,' Janet smiled as she stood briskly to her feet. 'The doctor should be here soon, and Luke will be eager for your company this morning. There wasn't much opportunity for the two of you to be alone together last night.'

It was almost eleven o'clock before Emma considered Luke free to entertain Shelley. The doctor had been and gone an hour before, but there had been physiotherapy and medication to administer, and then she hadn't been able to refrain from voicing mild disapproval of any prolonged discussions or undue emotional strain for her patient.

'Super-efficient,' Luke confided wryly as he viewed Shelley across the small table separating them out on the screened verandah. He reached out a hand to lift a glass of fruit juice to his lips and drank with evident satisfaction.

'I had noticed,' Shelley sparkled impishly. 'I fear

she has the makings of becoming something of a martinet in years to come.'

'All this gave you a bit of shock, I daresay.'

She looked at him with a measure of sadness, and her eyes were particularly eloquent. 'I wish I'd known. I would have come home before this.'

'You're here now,' he said gently. 'That's what counts.'

'The garden is looking grand,' she offered a trifle sadly. 'I went out this morning, and there's not a weed in sight.'

'You love this house and its surrounding cane-fields almost as much as I do,' he stated, viewing the gently-sloping land stretched out before him in a softly-swaying carpet of lush green cane. 'I want you to know that you've been well taken care of. And don't look at me like that. Smile, young Shelley. I've had more joy and happiness than any one man deserves in a lifetime.' There was a suspicion of a twinkle in those dark eyes as he queried softly, 'Do you want me to sit around all day with tears in my eyes just because I'm going to die?'

'Of course not,' she denied shakily.

'If I have to look at your sad face, we'll both end up weeping on each other's shoulder.' He smiled devilishly. 'Then the good Emma will forbid me your company. Can't have that.'

'You're every bit as bad as Mitch,' Shelley declared with mock despair.

'Been teasing you again, has he?'

'I sometimes have difficulty retaining my sense of humour,' she offered wryly.

'He rattles you, in other words?'

'And bullies me,' she twinkled unrepentantly. 'In

his eyes, I'm forever sixteen and a veritable babe in the bush!'

Luke began to chuckle. 'Comparing his experience with yours, I'm inclined to agree with him.'

'That's a backhanded compliment, if ever there was one!'

'Ever consider he might be biding his time?' Luke shot speculatively, and his eyes were suddenly alert.

'Why should he do that?' she asked slowly.

'Why indeed, young Shelley?' he mused idly. 'It's the only thing I regret.'

Shelley answered softly, 'Grandchildren. I imagine Janet will have her hands full in a few years' time.'

Luke grinned amiably. 'This house is big enough, for it was built with several children in mind. Fate decreed only two—my son, Cathie's daughter. Let's hope the next generation will be more generously blessed.'

'Cathie loved it here,' she said simply.

'She was a beautiful woman, with that rare quality—a truly beautiful soul,' he accorded quietly. 'Those five years we had together were the sweetest a man could hope for. I thank God that I was privileged to share a part of her life.'

The tears in her eyes were a physical ache, and there wasn't one word she could have uttered just then.

'Remember the first day you arrived here, Shelley?' he reflected quizzically.

'Yes.' She managed a watery smile. 'I was so overawed that I couldn't speak for days.'

He began to laugh in remembrance. 'You were

like a spaniel puppy the day it opened its eyes for the very first time.'

'To find itself in the lap of luxury, with an affectionate welcome that came straight from the heart,' she added softly.

'Ah, child. You returned it, twofold.' He closed his eyes as if memories had suddenly become painful. 'Play the guitar for me, Shelley,' he bade after a long silence, and when she fetched it he listened without once opening his eyes. After a while she faltered, thinking he had fallen asleep, but his voice urged her to continue.

Lunch was at midday, and in spite of a faint feeling of unease at the start of the meal when she met the carefully bland expression in Mitch's tawny eyes, there was nothing in his manner to give hint to the anger she had aroused the previous evening. If anything, he seemed to direct most of his attention towards Emma, who preened visibly with delight.

'I'm driving into Mossman for an hour or so,' Mitch indicated genially as she began clearing dishes from the table. 'Care to come along for the ride, young Shelley?'

Ordinarily she would have jumped at the chance, but a few things rankled—especially the 'young Shelley' tag! There was no reason why she shouldn't go. Luke took a siesta until four in the afternoon, and Emma had firmly forbidden anyone to enter his room on the grounds that he was supposed to nap as well as rest.

'Sorry, Mitch,' she said without a semblance of regret, and knew from the slight narrowing of his eyes that he was wholly aware of the reason behind her refusal. Good! One female in the house openly fawning for his attention was quite sufficient. 'With

Louise, Lynn and Hal arriving tomorrow, Janet will need some help.' She met his gaze squarely, offering him a sweet smile. 'I'll be busy baking most of the afternoon.'

'Far be it that such a hive of industry should be prevented,' he drawled quizzically, and Shelley bristled at the lazy gleam in his eyes.

True, she almost capitulated when the last dish had been dried and put away, but the faintly teasing manner he adopted on his way out settled it.

'Sure you won't change your mind, little one?'

Little one! When would he ever admit she was a young woman of twenty years, barely weeks away from her twenty-first birthday—an *adult*. She didn't trust herself to speak and simply shook her head.

Janet, bless her, didn't make any comment, but the look she flashed Mitch was telling, and her very silence indicated disapproval.

'You think I should have gone, don't you?' Shelley asked with her usual candour.

Janet turned from her task of greasing oven trays ready to receive spoonfuls of the biscuit mixture Shelley had just prepared, and regarded the younger girl steadily.

'You're a very intelligent girl, Shelley, and I love you dearly,' she began with a measure of exasperation. 'But there are times when you don't make any attempt to recognise what's beneath your very nose!'

Shelley felt immeasurably hurt. 'You're talking in riddles, Janet,' she began unevenly. 'Ever since I arrived home there's been some sort of conspiracy going on. You needn't worry—I've guessed what it's about.'

Janet uttered a pent-up sigh that defied description. 'Knowing you and that unprecedented streak 'of independence, your guess is bound to be about as accurate as predicting a rainstorm in the desert.'

'It's remarkably simple,' Shelley said slowly.

'It is,' Janet agreed in a rush before Shelley could continue. 'However, it's not for me to say.'

Shelley breathed in deeply in an effort to calm her jangling nerves. 'In that case, let's change the subject,' she determined sagely, and having emptied the contents of the mixing bowl on to two trays, she began collecting ingredients for the next batch. 'Where are Louise, Lynn and Hal going to sleep?'

'Mitch is giving up his room to Hal—he'll use the divan in the study—Louise and Lynn will occupy the remaining guest room,' Janet told her abstractedly as she sprinkled icing sugar on top of a sponge she had baked before lunch.

For the following two hours they worked diligently, sharing an easy silence for the most part, and there was a mutual satisfaction when the last tray was taken from the oven.

'Now, for the worst part—the dishes!' Shelley grinned, her humour restored.

'There's nothing like happy chatter from the kitchen, together with the tantalising smell of fresh baking,' a deep drawl mused from the doorway. 'Makes a mere man aware how necessary is the female of the species.'

'Necessary for his creature comforts,' Shelley sallied with spirit, and couldn't resist pulling a face at him.

Mitch moved into the kitchen and stood regarding the fruits of their labours with an appreciative smile. Idly, he reached out a hand and touched her cheek. 'Flour,' he explained solemnly, then reached for an iced biscuit.

'You'll get fat,' she declared impudently, knowing it to be a downright lie. Broad-boned he undoubtedly was, but hard work and a seemingly inexhaustible supply of energy ensured that not a spare ounce of flesh sat anywhere on that hard muscular frame.

His light chuckle was her undoing and she grinned amiably, knowing their former camaraderie to be restored.

- 'You could well do with a few extra pounds,' he teased lightly, and taking a bite from the biscuit he had selected, popped the remaining half into her mouth. 'Being fashionably slender is one thing, but a man prefers something more substantial than a delicate bundle of skin and bone in his arms.'

'We can't all be great buxom specimens,' she complained. 'In any case, not all men share your sentiments regarding the female form.'

'Ah, but mine are the only ones you need bother about, little one.'

For a moment his words startled her, then confusion brought a rush of colour to her cheeks so that she hurriedly bent her head and began filling empty tins with unnecessary haste.

'I don't know how you manage to work that out,' she muttered almost beneath her breath.

'You will.' There was no amusement in his voice, just calm assurance, and Shelley had an overwhelming desire to resort to a childish display of temper.

He really was the limit! she fumed inwardly. Hinting at something she daren't even think about, expecting her to know exactly what he meant without clarifying it.

'You should be careful who you say things like that to,' she managed wryly. 'One of your many girlfriends just might take you seriously.'

'Do you think that's possible?'

Anger sparked her eyes alive as she rounded on him in total exasperation. 'Mitchell Ballantyne, don't you have any work to do?'

'A firebreak to organise, mechanical equipment to check,' he replied easily. 'I had hoped my visit to the kitchen would bring an offer of tea. The men have stopped for smoko.'

'Good heavens,' Janet exclaimed in dismay. 'It can't be half past three already? No wonder you're thirsty!'

'It is, and I am.'

Shelley had the grace to look abashed. 'Leave the dishes, Janet. I'll make the tea.'

It was just as Mitch was about to place his drained cup back on to its saucer some ten minutes later that he issued the command that she be ready shortly before nine that evening.

'Luke will have gone to bed by then,' he elaborated. 'I have to go over to the Parellis' to deliver a spare part for their mechanical harvester.'

'Why take me along? I'll only cramp your style,' Shelley argued obliquely.

In one lithe movement he unbent his lengthy frame from the table, pushed in his chair, then stood regarding her sardonically. 'If I thought you'd do that, I wouldn't ask you to come.'

'You didn't ask—you ordered me to be ready.'

'Since when have you taken to splitting proverbial hairs?' His voice was a silk-smooth drawl and it sent shivers down her spine.

'I'm not a child any more,' she retorted.

'No,' he agreed sombrely. 'But I doubt you're ready to be treated as a woman.'

'If being treated as a woman amounts to being bullied, I think I'll take a raincheck.'

His eyes hardened until they resembled chips of gleaming topaz. 'Stop it right there, little one,' he advised dangerously, and turned on his heel.

'Shelley, Shelley,' Janet chided uneasily the moment Mitch left the kitchen. 'What ails you, child?'

'Nothing, everything—oh, I don't know,' Shelley muttered shakily. 'I can't seem to help it.'

'Take my advice and don't antagonise him. He's a man slow to anger, but once he's roused I'd be fearful of the consequences.'

'Beware of the sleeping tiger,' she declared absently.

'Something like that,' Janet agreed with the beginnings of a smile. 'Make your peace over dinner, and go with him.'

Shelley did, but from all appearances it seemed she needn't have bothered, for Mitch blandly declared their intended outing as everyone gathered in the lounge after dinner. Luke's enthusiastic approval, likewise Janet's, left her little option. Emma's quickly-veiled lashes and slightly-thinned lips were momentary, but Shelley doubted anyone other than herself witnessed it.

'One does tend to become slightly bored having to remain in the house,' Emma pointed out sweetly, giving Mitch a stunning smile. 'I always look forward to my weekends off.'

Mitch merely smiled that slow attractive smile of his and turned his attenton to Shelley.

'Fetch both guitars, child,' he bade quietly.

'Both?' she queried with uncertainty, for it wasn't often he professed a desire to play in company.

57

His eyes gleamed with sudden humour as he sensed the slight anxiety in her voice. 'Both, Shelley,' he assured her with deliberate emphasis.

He darned well would, wouldn't he? she cursed silently.

An accomplished guitarist himself, it had been Mitch who had encouraged her to take lessons, and during her early teenage years had proved himself a hard taskmaster. His tutorage paid off, as he had known it would, for she possessed a natural ear for music and played with sensitivity. Her voice was simply an added bonus.

On her return to the lounge she handed him his instrument with a dubious glance. If he chose anything difficult she'd never forgive him!

She needn't have worried, for he had evidently decided to treat her gently, and after tuning, played the more intricate lead, thus leaving her to follow. As always, she never ceased to be surprised that such obviously masculine hands could evoke the beautiful sounds that flowed at his fingers' touch. His own particular forte verged from semi-classical to the incredibly difficult classical exercises, although he rarely executed these for ears other than his own.

Now, he seemed content to drift from one country-and-western melody to another, and lifted a quizzical eyebrow when she shook her head in refusal to his request that she sing.

It was the kind of evening they had often shared in musical entertainment when Cathie was alive, twice, perhaps three times a week. There had been laughter when forgotten words refused readily to come to mind, or in Shelley's case, a wrong chord played. For there was no television mast close enough to enable an adequate reception during those early years, and invariably they played cards, chess, indulged in lengthy discussions on anything that held their interest, and listened to music.

It was all of an hour before Mitch placed his guitar to one side and flexed his powerful shoulders.

'Most enjoyable,' Luke declared with immense pleasure, and his kindly brown eyes gleamed warmly as they embraced first Shelley, then his son.

Janet looked up from her needlework and added a smiling endorsement as Emma provided an irritating note by showering obsequious praise on Mitch's undaunted head.

'I had absolutely no idea you could play so well,' she exclaimed enthusiastically. 'Why, you could easily make your fortune—Mitchell Ballantyne, guitarist and balladeer. People would simply flock to see and hear you.'

'My dear, he already possesses a fortune,' Luke essayed with a certain amount of wry cynicism.

And from Mitch—'I hate to disillusion you, but I don't sing at all.'

Shelley pulled a face at him and laughed, 'With a voice like yours, trying to keep in tune is sheer murder!'

'Good heavens, that's hard to believe,' Emma protested sharply, throwing Mitch a sympathetic smile. 'Your speaking voice is so deeply modulated, it should be perfect for singing.'

Shelley's eyes fairly danced with impudence. 'Therein lies the problem!'

Mitch cast her a glance that promised retaliation. 'Whenever I do forget myself and burst into song, Shelley inevitably drops an octave and fights a losing battle to maintain it. She then see-saws rather alarmingly between the two—an effect which is not exactly melodious,' he slanted laconically.

'Just for that,' Shelley twinkled unrepentantly, 'I've a good mind to stay at home and let you go to the Parellis' alone.'

'Not a chance, little one,' he drawled. 'Go put a comb through your hair or whatever, while I help Emma get Luke into bed.'

In her room, she changed her skirt and top for a fashionable below-the-knee-length skirt that was made up of several alternate bias-cut lengths of material sewn together obliquely, and slipped on a scarlet fabric-knit top. Her hair she simply brushed back behind her ears and caught it together at her nape with a scarf in matching scarlet. Wedge-heeled strap sandals completed the outfit, and Shelley stood back from the mirror feeling well pleased with the overall effect. A touch of lipstick, eyeliner, subtle use of eyeshadow and mascara took only a few minutes, and she was ready. Quickly she added a dab of perfume behind each ear, to the base of her throat and at each wrist before moving out down the hall to the lounge.

As she expected Mitch was waiting, albeit patiently, and his warm ready smile did strange things to her breathing. He too had changed, and looked rugged and invincible in beige suede trousers and a short-sleeved body-shirt of dark tan.

'I think the Brisbane fashion scene is somewhat ahead of our small country community, young Shelley,' he murmured speculatively. 'The Parelli girls will be envious, and Roberto will undoubtedly be stunned into speechlessness.'

'That's a gross exaggeration, Mitch,' she twinkled, and then began to laugh. 'I'm only trying to even things up a bit. Your presence at the Parelli farm usually has a dazzling effect on each of the girls—they hang on to every word you utter.'

'Indeed, you are sparkling well tonight,' he drawled with amusement. 'I can see I'll have my work cut out keeping track of all those irrepressible impish witticisms you intend entertaining me with. In your present frame of mind, you'd be wise to refuse alcohol in any form.'

'Intent on playing big brother?'

The look he cast her held only the merest trace of humour. 'That sort of remark could well herald trouble of a kind you'd find hard to handle.'

'Not from you, Mitch,' she answered sweetly as she slipped into the front seat of the car. 'I'm *young* Shelley, and scarcely out of the schoolroom.'

The door shut with a firm decisive click, then he moved round to the other side and eased his lengthy frame in behind the wheel. Even in the car's dim interior the glitter in his eyes was evident.

'Cool it, little one. These past thirty-six hours you've been hell-bent on a path to self-destruction. Keep it up, and I'll help things along a bit,' he warned implacably as he put the car into gear.

'I'm sorry,' she apologised quietly when the silence between them had stretched to more than five minutes. There was little she could discern from his expression, and when he failed to acknowledge her words she viewed the windscreen with a mixture of remorse and despair. They were approaching Mossman township and the street lights spread their glow over numerous cars angle-parked from the kerb on the main street.

Shelley transferred her attention to the handkerchief she was nervously fingering. 'Don't go all

61

quiet and chilly on me, Mitch. I don't think I could bear it.'

A slow smile widened his mouth, sending deep creases curving up towards his cheekbone, and there was a teasing light in those dark tawny eyes. 'Chilly?'

'You're very good at displaying silent disapproval,' she voiced shakily.

'You make it sound like a common occurrence, when I can't readily recall more than a few instances,' he chided musingly.

'I have a vivid recollection of each and every one of them,' Shelley revealed bleakly.

His expression softened as he lifted a hand to her cheek and idly trailed warm fingers down to the curve of her chin. 'That bad?'

Her eyes searched his features, unaware of what she was seeking. 'You've been a devastating influence in my life. I don't quite know what I'll do without you,' she finished seriously.

His eyes never left the road for a second, and it seemed a long time before he queried gently, 'Has it never occurred to you that you mightn't have to?'

Oh, dear God, that thought had been a part of her days and nights for years! It took tremendous effort to smile, but she managed it. 'I don't imagine your future wife would be wildly ecstatic to have you share your affections.'

'Who said anything about sharing?' he parried mildly.

Shelley swallowed the lump that suddenly rose in her throat. 'I'd be careful to whom you say things like that,' she began hesitantly. 'Lots of girls would consider that tantamount to . . .' she faltered, unable to continue.

'A proposal?'

'Proposing what?' she asked abstractedly.

'Marriage. I wouldn't settle for less.'

Shelley felt way out of her depth and temporarily speechless.

'Lost for words, young Shelley?' his voice teased gently several minutes later.

'It's true, then?' she queried shakily, feeling completely enervated and sure that she would never smile again.

'That I'm contemplating marriage? Yes.'

The sooner they arrived at the Parelli farm, the better, she perceived wretchedly.

'At least tell me who she is so that I can extend my congratulations.' Was that her voice, so low as to be almost a whisper?

'I've a few arrangements to complete.' One hand left the wheel as he extracted cigarettes and matches from his shirt pocket. 'Give it a few days yet, Shelley.'

The Parelli farm was half-way between Mossman and Port Douglas, and some ten minutes later the car turned off the main road and deviated half a mile towards the coast.

Shelley hadn't offered a word by way of conversation, whereas Mitch had smoked two cigarettes with deliberate calm and given every indication of enjoying a companionable silence.

The farmhouse was ablaze with light, and no sooner had the car drawn to a halt than Mr and Mrs Parelli appeared on the verandah to welcome them, followed quickly by the rest of their family.

Mitch presented a fine example of expansive urbanity, accepting the wine Bruno Parelli offered, and soon the men were immersed in a discussion about machinery.

63

Smiling at Gianna's sigh of resignation, Shelley followed the girls into the lounge where fashion magazines, hair-styles and make-up filled the entire conversation.

Gianna, the eldest of the four sisters, was an attractive, vivacious girl with a warm ready smile, and Shelley reflected that she would make any man a good wife.

'Come out into the dining-room for coffee,' Mrs Parelli bade from the doorway over an hour later, and her request was greeted with enthusiasm.

Mitch was seated near the head of the table opposite Roberto, and his eyes twinkled with hidden humour as Gianna manipulated the seating arrangements so that Shelley sat next to her brother, while she herself took the coveted chair beside Mitch.

'You are pleased to be home?'

Shelley turned slightly and met Roberto's friendly gaze. 'Yes,' she answered simply. 'I wish it could have been under happier circumstances.'

'Ah, yes—Luke. You're very fond of him, aren't you?'

She nodded silently. 'He's a wonderful man.'

'Perhaps you'd care to come out with me one evening?'

Shelley glanced into those dark brown eyes not far from her own and saw the warmth reflected there. Why not? she mused idly. 'Thanks, Roberto, I'd like that.'

'Tomorrow?'

'Not so fast!' she laughed a little at his eager smile. 'We have Luke's sister and her son and daughter arriving tomorrow, and in any case I wouldn't go out until after Luke goes to bed, which is at nine o'clock.'

'We could have a few drinks in town,' he suggested. 'Thursday?'

'Ring me before dinner, and I'll let you know,' she promised kindly.

'What was all that about?'

Shelley felt an imp of mischief prompt her to tease him a little. 'Why, Mitch, what do you mean?'

The car slowed and turned on to the main road, then quickly gathered speed. It was late, almost midnight, and only the merest trace of burnt-off cane clung to the cool clear air.

'Roberto,' Mitch explained succinctly.

She shot him a quick look and felt the stirrings of anger begin. 'He asked me out, and I accepted. Any objection?'

'Don't encourage him, little one. It wouldn't be fair.'

'Fair!' she cried angrily. 'What has that got to do with it?'

'Go out with him by all means,' he replied steadily. 'But you'll have me to reckon with if you employ any bewitching tactics.'

'Mitchell Ballantyne! I'm free to go out with whoever I choose, and what's more, your days as self-appointed protector are over.' She tossed her head angrily and then pushed back long strands of hair that had fallen across her cheek. 'I'm almost twenty-one, and well able to take care of myself!'

'Shelley, Shelley,' he chided softly. 'You're creating a storm in a teacup.'

'I am? I thought that was your prerogative.'

He began to chuckle, and the sound of that deep voice caught up with humour was her undoing.

'I shan't ever speak to you again,' she declared unevenly.

'Until tomorrow,' he mused wryly.

Shelley maintained an injured silence throughout the rest of the drive home, and her throat ached with suppressed emotion. Somehow, she had to get through the next few weeks without becoming too much of a nervous wreck, although how she was going to achieve such a miracle was unknown! Once Mitch made up his mind to do something, he invariably acted swiftly, and she didn't doubt that he would declare his intention to marry and disclose the girl's identity within the next few days. In all probability he would present his intended bride with an engagement ring one day and hurry her to church the next!

The homestead was in darkness except for two lights illuminating the verandah, and she quickly opened her door as soon as Mitch brought the car to a halt.

'Goodnight,' she bade him with quiet civility, and was mortified to hear his voice in mocking reply.

'Pleasant dreams, little one.'

## CHAPTER FOUR

THE morning was caught up with changing bed-linen and the inumerable tasks Janet deemed necessary to set the house gleaming like a new pin. It was never less than spotless, thanks to her dedicated efforts, and little escaped her critical eye. The furniture was gracefully old and polished to within an inch of its life, as were the vinyl floor coverings. But with the expectation of visitors, each last wisp of dust was ousted from every nook and cranny.

Shelley was glad of the activity, for it meant she didn't have time to mull over Mitch's elusive innuendoes. His expression at lunch had been one of bland affability, and if anything seemed to direct most of his attention towards Emma, who reacted with sickening animation.

A dormant shaft of jealousy shot to the surface that quite destroyed Shelley's appetite, and as soon as the dishes had been dealt with, she changed into shorts and a halter top, then escaped out into the garden to weed with determined dedication.

There was something infinitely satisfying about tending the well-cared-for shrubs and flowers, nipping off withered blooms, witnessing the exquisite beauty of nature. Such glorious colour and perfect symmetry never ceased to arouse her admiration.

'What in sweet hell do you think you're doing?'

Shelley's hands halted in their task and remained poised a few inches above the rich dark soil. The sound of that low-pitched drawl was enough to raise her blood-pressure to a point of mercurial anger. With careful effort she sat back on her heels and shielded her eyes from the strong sunlight as she glanced upwards.

'I don't imagine hell could possibly be sweet,' she retorted with asperity. 'As to what I'm doing—I would have thought that was obvious.'

'The time for gardening is early morning, as you know only too well,' Mitch slanted grimly. 'I have enough to contend with as it is, without the addition of sunstroke.'

'My head is adequately covered,' she maintained reasonably.

67

His husky oath was barely audible. 'A scrap of a scarf that neither shields your face nor protects your neck. On your feet, little one,' he commanded brusquely.

'When I've finished,' she countered evenly, returning to her task. Darn his overbearing manner! He could jolly well practise his superiority on his unknown fiancée—no doubt she would revel in it!

'If you aren't on your feet ten seconds from now,' he warned with dangerous calm, 'you'll discover just how unsweet hell can be.'

Capitulation was obviously the only course she could take, and she stood gracefully upright, her expressive features stormy and resentful. To antagonise him further would undoubtedly bring retribution, and she had no desire to have Luke, perchance he was awake, witness them quarrelling.

'I'll fetch a hat,' she offered, half-turning away, only to have her arm caught in a bruising grip.

'No hat,' he advised softly.

Shelley met those tawny eyes and inwardly blanched at the total implacability evident in their depths. It seemed useless to explain that she hadn't intended to stay out in the garden very long, and no good at all to pretend ignorance over the dangers of the sun's rays in this tropical climate.

'I'd have thought that after this morning's activity you would have had the sense to rest for an hour,' Mitch began evenly as she fell into step beside him —not that she had much choice to do otherwise. 'All your sane, sensible instincts seem to have flown the coop,' he mused tolerantly. 'I wonder why?'

'Maybe I finally baulked at being treated like a child?' she parried significantly.

'Prove you're all grown up, and I'll change my tactics.'

'I'm thoroughly tired of your "big brother" attitude,' she flung furiously, coming to a halt beside the jacaranda. His grip on her arm didn't lessen and she attempted to pull free with little success. 'Everything I say and do seems to amuse you, and you never ask—you *command*,' she finished shakily as she eyed the muscular arm that reached out to lean against the tree providing an inescapable barrier. He seemed dangerously close, and there was an indefinable emotion smouldering from the depths of his eyes as his head bent down to hover within inches of her own.

She made one last desperate attempt to elude him and failed miserably. His mouth was relentlessly hard and there seemed never to be an end to the intense pressure as he moulded her slim curves to his hard frame.

'You deserved that,' he declared ruthlessly, releasing his hold a mere fraction as he gazed down at her tearfilled eyes and quivering bruised lips. 'Just for the record, my intentions are far from brotherly.' His lips descended and she braced herself against a further onslaught.

It never came. Instead, his mouth teased hers, gently at first, then with an increasing passion as her response came unbidden, and it was he who disentangled her arms timeless minutes later and stood back to regard her in silence.

'This is hardly the time or place,' Mitch said quietly, catching a hold of her hand in his. 'Smoko time, Shelley. If I ask, not command, will you make a cup of tea?'

There was the faintest smile twisting the edge of

his mouth, his eyes warm, and her heart flipped rather crazily. 'Of course,' she smiled, totally bemused.

'Perhaps I should kiss you more often,' he teased lightly.

Shelley's smile broadened. 'You've managed it a few times in the past three days. Making the most of your freedom?'

'Oh, I'd plan on having it become a regular occurrence, young Shelley.' Carefully measured words that upset her equilibrium so that she lapsed into silence as they stepped up on to the verandah and made their way to the kitchen.

It appeared that Janet had forestalled them, for the table was already set for four and she was in the process of pouring boiling water into the teapot.

'Tell Emma it's smoko time, there's a dear,' Janet bade with a smile, and Shelley disengaged her hand from Mitch's grasp.

There was a strange sort of excitement building up inside her, as if she was on the verge of a wonderful discovery, and any thoughts she might have on the subject were determinedly tucked away for future reference. 'Although heaven knows when I'll have any time to myself to think,' she muttered beneath her breath as she paused outside Emma's room.

'There's tea and something to eat ready in the kitchen, Emma,' she called from the open doorway, and at once the nurse stood to her feet.

'Just a drink,' Emma acknowledged without a semblance of a smile. Her glance took in Shelley's slightly bemused expression and her dark eyes seemed to glitter with animosity.

Why, for heaven's sake? Shelley pondered perplexedly. Admittedly they had little in common, but what possible reason could the girl have for obviously disliking her? Mitch was a probable cause, but even so ... Emma's room was on the wrong side of the house for her to have witnessed that scene in the garden, and in any case the jacaranda provided an adequate screen.

'We're to have visitors, I believe,' Emma commented as she walked beside Shelley down to the hall towards the kitchen.

'Yes. Luke's sister and her two children—well,' Shelley grinned companionably, 'scarcely children. Hal is around twenty-five, and Lynn is my age.'

Emma nodded non-committally. 'I must insist that no strain be placed on Mr Ballantyne. A houseful of visitors is not conducive to his quiet rest periods.'

If they hadn't reached the kitchen at that moment, Shelley would have burst into emphatic speech. What was the matter with the girl? Luke was mere weeks away from meeting his Maker, and should be permitted as many of his family around him as he wished! No one in their right mind would tire him, or overtax his limited strength in any way.

'Ah—come and have some tea,' Mitch adjured with a friendly smile. 'Janet has surpassed herself as usual, and there's an array of cakes as well as scones.'

Shelley could sense what the nurse was going to say before she spoke.

'Just tea, thank you,' Emma smiled winningly towards Mitch. 'I'm very much a health "nut", and eat only at mealtimes.'

His smile broadened a little as he reached for a well-buttered light fluffy scone. 'During the season

71

we need plenty of good food to provide sufficient energy.'

Emma accepted a cup of tea, declined sugar, and surveyed the well-laid table with disfavour. 'Energy can be derived from natural foods, which incidentally contain far less cholesterol and carbohydrate.'

'Perhaps,' he granted urbanely. 'But less satisfying to the taste-buds. Shelley looks in need of a few extra pounds. At a guess, I'd say she's been existing on yoghurt and fruit juices three times a day instead of eating adequate meals.'

'That's a downright injustice, Mitchell Ballantyne,' Shelley sprang immediately in defence.

'Leave her be, Mitch,' Janet chuckled, and changed the subject. 'What time did Ken leave for Cairns?'

He drained his cup and reached for the teapot, pouring a second cup and spooning sugar into it before answering. 'An hour ago. He wanted sometime up his sleeve—a few calls he had to make on the way in.'

'He doesn't change,' Shelley mused thoughtfully, recalling Ken Pemberton's friendly face to mind. 'I must slip down and see him,' she added remorsefully. 'He'll be thinking I've forgotten him.'

Mitch eyed her thoughtfully. 'Why would he think that, young Shelley? He's aware of the situation here.'

'Bake him a cake, and take it down after lunch tomorrow,' Janet suggested.

'I must get back.' Emma stood to her feet in one graceful movement. 'Mr Ballantyne will wake soon.'

'Likewise,' Mitch smiled easily, following her example, and Shelley's eyes followed them as they left the kitchen together. Even seeing him in the girl's company was enough to cause the little green monster to stir restlessly inside her. He was so tall, so solid and indomitable—the mainstay of her existence.

'What have you planned for dinner, Janet?' she queried prosaically in an attempt to redirect her thoughts.

'Consommé, roast fillet of beef with roast potatoes and two greens, followed by cheesecake and fruit salad,' Janet answered meditatively. 'Perhaps I'll pop some pumpkin and carrots into the roasting pan as well.'

'Delicious.' Shelley stood to her feet and stretched with an almost feline grace. 'I'll prepare the vegetables and——' she paused in speculation, '—perhaps I'll make an apple strudel for supper.'

They worked happily side by side for more than an hour, then took a brief respite to drink lemonade from cool frosted glasses. Shelley spent a brief thirty minutes with Luke—all that Emma would permit in view of an influx of visitors—then quickly showered and changed before returning to the kitchen.

She heard Mitch enter the house and go through to the study—he would already have showered in the outhouse a few steps from the back door that held a laundry and an extra bathroom. Even with mechanical harvesters there was still a measurable amount of soot from the burnt-off cane that managed to creep on to the men's working clothes and infiltrate through to their skin.

Very soon Ken would arrive with Luke's sister and Hal and Lynn. Louise was quite outspoken, often bluntly so, but likeable nonetheless, and Lynn was a pleasant girl with an effervescent personality.

73

Hal, Shelley regarded with caution. He was a flirt who regarded any uninterested female as a challenge —the more unattainable, the more persistent he tended to become. It was little wonder his marriage of two years had recently ended in separation.

There was only the table to set, and she had just stood back to check everything was in place when there was the muted sound of car doors slamming and voices raised in greeting.

Louise looked exactly as she had the previous time she had visited, almost a year ago; the two-piece suit a replica of one worn then, only this time it was in a soft shade of blue. Her hair had been tinted a pale lavender and was coiffured in its usual short wavy style. To Louise Cartwright the changing fashions meant merely the taking up or letting down of a hemline. In the ten years Shelley had known her, Louise always travelled in a two-piece suit, and wore a button-through smock inside the house.

Fortunately Lynn hadn't inherited her mother's uniform sense of dress, and displayed a preference for up-to-date designs and colours that showed her rather ordinary features to their best advantage.

Hal, on the other hand, was impeccably groomed to the point where one expected a photographer to suddenly appear and request a specific pose, such was his stance.

Shelley suppressed a prankish wish that she might get dust on his trousers, or a little grease on his shirt—no man deserved to look as he did, *all* of the time. He resembled a superior male model on show, and in fact he did earn a living in this trade, travelling extensively throughout the country modelling clothes.

'You look thinner, child,' Louise greeted her

without preamble, and Shelley managed a smile, for to take umbrage at any of Louise's remarks would have meant being in a permanent state of pique.

'I wear the same size clothes as I did a year ago, Louise,' she replied steadily.

'You look ravishing,' Hal commended, his eyes running over her slim figure with a practised gleam.

'Yes, doesn't she?' Mitch agreed with amused indulgence, placing a casual arm about her shoulders. 'The duckling has without doubt become a beautiful swan.'

'Any time you want to earn some real money, just let me know,' Hal drawled speculatively. 'As a model you'd be sensational.'

'It's as well I never take either of you seriously,' Shelley declared evenly.

'Still the same old Mitch,' Lynn grinned contentedly as she stepped up on to the verandah.

'I'll give Ken a hand with the luggage,' Mitch declared, and suited words to action.

Luke joined them in the lounge for a drink, and whatever reservations he might have regarding his nephew his welcome was genuinely warm.

'What has been happening in your little world, Shelley?'

Shelley took time to sip the contents of her glass before turning slightly to meet Hal's frankly sensuous gaze. One needed to arm oneself with some kind of protection against Hal, and her cool wit usually sufficed to keep him at a distance. Although conversing with him was akin to a verbal fencing match!

'Oh, this and that,' she replied gaily.

'Elaborate, Shelley dear—you're being horribly evasive,' he drawled idly.

She pulled a slight face at him and managed a creditable smile. 'I can't imagine you'd be interested in the antics of small children and their education.'

He reached out a hand and touched a long strand of hair that lay over her shoulders. 'Oh, I don't know. It could prove fascinating.'

'It very often is,' Shelley declared solemnly, deliberately moving back a pace. 'I find it extremely rewarding.'

'There are more rewarding things in life,' Hal mocked softly.

'Of course,' she agreed, albeit sweetly.

His eyes roved intimately over her expressive features and a slight smile played about his lips. 'Don't tell me the swan is spreading her wings at long last?'

'You'll never know, will you?' she countered easily, deliberately swinging away from him to capture Lynn's attention. In doing so she encountered Mitch's narrowed gaze, and her eyes widened guilelessly. He's watching me like a hawk, she perceived with idle interest—or rather, he's watching Hal! Somehow that cheered her, and the smile she directed towards Lynn was quite something.

'How's the world of commercial art?' she queried lightheartedly.

'Fabulous. You know that I'm freelancing now?' Lynn said warmly, and her expressive features brightened into an engaging grin.

'No, I didn't. Do you work at home, or do you have a studio?'

Lynn laughed. 'Oh, a studio. You know Mother— I'd never get anything done in between numerous cups of tea and cosy little chats!'

'Have you brought a sketching pad with you?'

'Yes,' the other girl declared. 'The garden here is really beautiful. I took colour photographs last time, but it's not the same.'

Shelley espied Janet slipping towards the door. 'I'll go and help Janet dish dinner,' she excused lightly.

It was a pleasant meal, at times quite amusing, for Hal deliberately set out to charm Emma, who in turn cast the occasional pleading glance towards Mitch. His reciprocal smile was charm itself, and there was none of the musing indulgence he afforded Shelley and Lynn.

'Play the guitar for me, Shelley.'

She glanced across at Luke, surprise evident in her clear smoky-blue eyes. They were all seated comfortably in the lounge enjoying an after-dinner drink, and she hadn't expected Luke to make the request. Her playing was very much a family thing for his enjoyment, and she felt ill at ease at the prospect of providing entertainment.

'Are you sure?' she queried gently. 'The others would probably prefer to talk instead of listening to me.'

'Dear Shelley, they're here to pander my dying wishes,' he twinkled wickedly. 'I have the advantage, so why not make use of it?'

'You're incorrigible, do you know that?' she chided laughingly.

'Tomorrow,' he declared. 'No matter what Emma says about physiotherapy and adequate rest, come along to my room in the morning—I'll handle any fuss she'll make. Now, fetch that guitar, child,' he bade lightly.

It wasn't exactly an easy half-hour, for she was acutely aware of Mitch's inscrutable expression,

Hal's eloquent gaze, and Emma's silent animosity. She felt so *exposed*, kneeling at Luke's feet, the centre of attention, and her usual enchantment with the music eluded her. The desire to escape from the room reflected itself in her expressive eyes, and she cast a rather desperate glance towards Janet, who, bless her, came immediately to the rescue.

'It's been a long day,' that good lady began. 'Shall we have coffee now?'

Shelley seized upon the opportunity with alacrity, declaring that she would see to its preparation before anyone had a chance to demur.

In the kitchen she made ready the tea-wagon while the percolator bubbled merrily, and taking the apple strudel from its tin she quickly prepared the icing. Now, only cake-forks to place on the wagon—the strudel to slice, and by then the coffee would be ready.

'Quite shockingly domesticated, aren't you?'

Shelley felt a pang of dismay at the sound of that dry sardonic voice close behind her—too close, she thought wryly as she turned to face him.

'Come to make yourself useful, Hal?' she queried coolly.

'Delighted,' he slanted significantly, bending his face to within touching distance of her own.

Shelley breathed in deeply and fixed him an icy glare. 'Halburton Cartwright, my fingers are all sticky with vanilla icing, and believe me, I won't hesitate to place them on your immaculate shirt as I push you out of the way. Two seconds,' she ended threateningly.

'All right, all right.' He hastily moved out of her reach, raising his hands defensively in the air. 'No need to act the outraged virgin. What harm is there in a friendly cousinly kiss?'

'I'm not your cousin, and your passes are rarely friendly,' she retorted, rinsing her hands beneath the tap.

'You don't know what you're mising.'

'I'd prefer to miss you entirely!' Honestly, the sheer conceit of him! she thought furiously as she all but thumped the percolator down on to the tea-wagon. Without a backward glance she wheeled it along the hall to the lounge.

If anyone noticed the twin flags of colour high on each cheekbone, or the stormy glint in her eyes, they made no comment.

'Ah,' Louise's eyes lit up with pleasure at the sight of the tea-wagon's contents. 'Apple strudel, whipped cream for my coffee—I'll have to watch my waistline!'

'Mother, you gave up on that years ago,' her daughter accused without rancour. 'Heaven knows where you put it all, for you never seem to gain an ounce.'

'Far too busy for it to settle any place,' Louise declared complacently.

'It's common knowledge that most people eat far too much,' Emma offered knowledgeably.

Fortunately any further comments Emma might have made were forestalled with the partaking of supper, and in no time at all she declared it to be Luke's bedtime.

Conversation after that seemed to centre around Louise's various social activities and the demands they made on her time. When Mitch returned after assisting Luke to bed, the talk became more general until almost eleven when everyone retired for the night.

Luke was as good as his word, although the disgruntled words Emma flung at Shelley indicated that she was directly responsible for Luke's obstinacy.

'I don't mean to overtire him,' Shelley assured her with a measure of patience.

'Whatever your intentions, your mere presence will prove a strain on his resources,' Emma returned curtly.

'Don't you think you might not be taking too much on yourself? Surely Luke's wishes at a time like this should count for something?'

'I'm employed to ensure that Mr Ballantyne has adequate rest and to supervise his medication,' Emma returned sharply.

'And his happiness means nothing?'

'I would have thought his health has first priority.'

'Not if the restrictions imposed on him rankle to a point where he's unhappy,' Shelley replied steadily, more angry than she cared to admit.

Emma's lips thinned to an unpleasant smile and her dark eyes glittered in a manner that boded ill for any adversary. 'I shall report your lack of consideration to Mitch.'

'Do that.' Without giving Emma a chance to say anything further, Shelley turned abruptly and left the lounge.

By the time she reached Luke's room she had regained control of her temper, and the smile she flashed him was affectionately warm.

'How do you feel this morning?'

'Better for seeing you,' Luke grinned, unabashed.

He held out his hand and motioned that she sit close beside the bed.

'The feeling is mutual,' she assured him, laughing. 'Now, what shall we talk about?'

'You.'

'Why? There's plenty of more interesting things to discuss, Luke,' she answered lightly.

He smiled a little and reached out to touch her hand. 'Have you any ideas, I wonder, of the pleasure you've given me these past ten years? This will always be your home for as long as you choose, Shelley. I'm aware how much you value your independence, which is why I've ensured that you can continue to be independent.' He paused momentarily and grinned rather wickedly as he witnessed her consternation at the outrageously large sum he revealed.

'You can't, Luke!' she protested earnestly. To be bequeathed such an amount was out of the question, and in any case it formed part of an inheritance that belonged to Mitch by right of birth.

'I can, and have,' he answered swiftly, and it wasn't her imagination that he looked very tired and strained in the bright morning light.

'How can you say that?'

'Shelley, Shelley,' Luke shook his head in mild rebuke. 'Mitch isn't being done out of anything—he's been a financial partner for the past ten years and retains a share equal to that of my own.'

She swallowed the lump that suddenly rose to her throat, and it was several seconds before she could find voice. 'The amounts I receive quarterly through the bank more than supplement my salary.'

Luke's eyes twinkled merrily. 'Those are merely interest from an investment I gifted Cathie shortly after our marriage,' he enlightened her. 'Transferred into your name when she died.'

'I never knew—why didn't you tell me?' she whispered.

'It was never important until now,' Luke answered.

'But I can't accept such an amount,' she argued, genuinely upset.

'How can you not accept something that's already been yours for the past five years?' he queried mildly.

'Does Mitch know about all this?' she asked doubtfully.

'Of course.'

'And he agrees?'

Luke began to chuckle, and his eyes fairly danced at her incredulous expression. 'It's at Mitch's instigation that I'm telling you now, rather than leave you to find out later.'

'I shall only gift it back,' she warned seriously.

'Impossible,' he stated musingly. 'There's a condition that it can't be passed back into Mitch's hands. Even if you never touched a cent, it would all eventually be inherited by your children,' he revealed gently. 'I'm an exceedingly wealthy man, child. Indulge me a little. Am I not entitled to die content that you'll be financially secure?'

'I'm not sure that I'll accept, just the same,' she reiterated mildly.

'You will—I insist. Would you upset me and hasten my demise?'

Shelley looked clearly horrified. 'Of course not!'

His smile was entirely satisfying. 'Good. We shall now forget about the whole thing. Play the guitar for me, Shelley.'

'You're almost as bad as Mitch,' she choked fiercely.

'A family failing, no doubt,' he chuckled, not in the least contrite.

'A law unto yourselves,' Shelley amended with quiet emphasis.

'Perhaps, in the sense that we both go after what we want with relentless forbearance.'

'That's an understatement! I can never win an argument against Mitch, either,' she essayed forlornly.

'Go fetch your guitar, child, and play for me,' he bade, his voice weary, and she immediately sprang to her feet and went to his side.

'Oh, Luke, I sound an ungrateful wretch,' she began remorsefully. 'And I'm not at all. I love you dearly,' she assured him as she hugged him affectionately.

'I know it,' he returned complacently. 'Now, play, Shelley. I find it soothes me.'

She played until his head drooped tiredly, and then sat silently, lost in reflective thought until a light tap at the door disturbed her reverie.

'You're wanted on the telephone,' Janet told her quietly, and Shelley quickly stood to her feet and followed Janet into the hall.

'Who is it?'

'Roberto Parelli,' Janet replied with a smile as she moved towards the kitchen.

'I'll be down soon to help,' Shelley called, then picked up the receiver.

It was indeed Roberto, wanting to know if she would go out with him that evening.

'Well——' Shelley deliberated, not sure that an evening away from the homestead mightn't be a good idea. 'All right, Roberto,' she agreed. 'Can you pick me up about nine?'

Out of the corner of her eye she saw Mitch enter the house via the side verandah, and as he moved into the hall Emma intercepted him. Shelley deliberately turned away so that she couldn't see what transpired, under no illusion that Emma was relating verbatim their exchange earlier this morning and perhaps adding a few embellishments of her own.

When Shelley put the receiver down she felt slightly guilty over sounding so enthusiastic at the prospect of an evening out. It wasn't really fair to let Roberto think she was so keen, but the sight of Mitch's fair head bent low and Emma's rapt expression had spurred her on.

Louise was talking to Janet when she stepped into the kitchen. It transpired Lynn and Hal were languishing out on the verandah in the mid-morning heat. Shelley had to hide a smile—the onset of a tropical summer was a vast change from the winter they'd left in Sydney!

Somehow she half expected Mitch to make an appearance—Emma had had plenty of time to air her grievances, and as nursing aid was difficult to come by, Mitch would feel duty-bound to keep the peace. Knowing Mitch, he'd choose the time and place to issue a reprimand, and it would be when she least expected it. It might be a good idea to get out of the way for a few hours, and with this thought in mind she went in search of Lynn to suggest an afternoon in Mossman. Tomorrow, if Mitch was agreeable to her having the car, she could take Lynn to Cairns for the day. As long as they returned by mid-afternoon so that she could help Janet with dinner there shouldn't be any objection. Luke appeared to be tied up with Emma's ministrations for a greater part of the morning, then spent most of the afternoon resting.

The more Shelley thought about it, the more pleased she became. All in all, she could take care of the daylight hours with such a wealth of activity that there wouldn't be a chance to give much thought to Mitch. Swept along with the idea, she mentally planned a day on the Tableland visiting Tinaroo Falls Dam, and an excursion to Lake Barrine. They could take a picnic lunch and swim.

When she acquainted Lynn with her plans they were met with unveiled enthusiasm, and the only snag was Hal. Naturally, he insisted on being included. However, Shelley felt she could handle him, especially as Lynn would be there as well, and after all, what possible harm could he do? She was willing to suffer a few skirmishes fending off his advances—given the choice, she'd opt for the wide open spaces as against Emma's cloying, righteous manner any time!

By some miracle neither Lynn or Hal mentioned that Shelley intended driving them into Mossman after lunch, although Shelley had been sure it would come out in conversation. Not that Mitch would have refused permission for them to use the car—she didn't need to ask, if it came to that, but he would prefer to know their plans.

Mitch returned to the paddock very soon after lunch, and as soon as the dishes had been dealt with, Shelley informed Janet and Louise that they had the afternoon to themselves.

'We'll be back around four, Janet,' she intimated gaily, meeting the slightly curious gleam that good woman directed her, then blowing a light kiss Shelley left the room.

The spare keys to the Chrysler sedan, the utility pick-up truck, and the Range-Rover were kept in the study, and Shelley invaded that sanctum and removed the sedan keys from their hook on the wall. If Mitch needed transport this afternoon he would scarcely be stranded, she mused thoughtfully.

Lynn was enthusiastic as Shelley eased the large car out from the garage and sent it gliding smoothly down the driveway to the road.

'It's good to get out for a while,' Lynn began happily. 'Not that I'm bored on the farm,' she amended quickly. 'It was Mother's idea that Hal and I accompany her. Quite honestly, I felt it would have been better if she'd come alone, but she was adamant that Luke would want to see Hal and me as well. Fortunately, we both have the sort of jobs that enable us to get away fairly easily.'

Hal shifted position in the roomy rear seat, and Shelley caught a glimpse of his faintly bored profile in the rear vision mirror.

'Easy for you, Lynn. I just happened to be between assignments, otherwise I wouldn't be here.'

'Have you been back long?'

Shelley turned slightly to answer Lynn, taking her eyes momentarily from the road. 'Monday afternoon. Luke's illness came as a shock,' she intimated sadly. 'He always seemed so healthy.'

'He sees to it that he has the best of attention,' Hal drawled. 'Money talks, obviously.'

'Why not?' his sister retaliated mildly.

Mossman was a small town—sleepy, Hal indicated in faintly bored tones during their walk down the main street. Shelley bristled protectively, for

86

small it might be, but it was the humming centre which local farmers and townspeople depended upon to supply their necessities. In ten years it had changed little, with the addition of a modern hotel to brighten the landscape. The hotels with their bars provided a convivial atmosphere in which to quaff large quantities of ice-cold beer at the end of a long hard day. During the season there were always plenty of men frequenting the bars in the evening, although now there were fewer due to farm mechanisation. The days of cane gangs with machetes to deal with the burnt-off cane were over. Now there were mechanical harvesters which made short work of the daily cane tonnage, but there was still a necessity for men to operate the machines. They were largely Italians and Jugoslavs, mostly single, who alternately worked the cane and then moved on to the tobacco harvesting in the Mareeba/Dimbulah area on the Tableland. The money was good, but the hours long and arduous in the heat of the tropical sun. Many did it for a few years so that they could set themselves up in business down south.

Shelley endeavoured to see the dust-covered streets, the lack of varied brightly-modern shops through Lynn and Hal's eyes, and failed to find it anything other than interesting, even endearing. Perhaps it was a case of 'home is where the heart is', she mused thoughtfully.

'How about a drink? This heat is getting to me,' Hal's voice intruded a trifle petulantly.

'It's just barely spring,' Shelley grinned without a trace of sympathy. 'In the height of summer it verges close on a hundred and thirty degrees in the midday sun, and then some.'

'Which is precisely why I stay further south,' he returned with asperity.

'Oh, don't be a grump,' Lynn derided with sisterly lack of tact. 'If you wear man-made fibres that retain the heat, what else can you expect?'

Hal made a crushing reply that had no effect whatsoever on the irrepressible Lynn, and with dancing eyes Shelley led the way into the lounge of the nearest hotel.

All things being considered, it was a pleasant afternoon. Hal's good looks and fashionably-groomed figure drew some attention, especially from the opposite sex, and conscious of being in the limelight he became a scintillating companion.

Shelley had a shandy, then held out for Coca-cola, for it was obvious that Hal was in his element and would be difficult to shift for the next hour or so. Tomorrow she'd plump for Lake Barrine on the Tableland, instead of Cairns!

## CHAPTER FIVE

'Did you have a nice time?'

Shelley smiled happily at Janet's query, and carried on with the task of washing lettuce over the sink. 'Great. Lynn and I get on well together.'

'I gather they're resting?' Janet said with a smile, and Shelley laughed.

'The heat,' she explained succinctly. 'Louise as well?'

'I think she retired in self-defence,' Janet implied carefully.

'Let me guess—Emma delivered one of her lectures over afternoon smoko?' Shelley hazarded impishly, and began to laugh as Janet nodded in agreement. 'I should have been here.'

'So you should.'

'Oh dear—Mitch,' Shelley grimaced. 'Like that, is it?'

'What possessed you not to tell him you intended going into town?'

Shelley sighed. 'He's going to be even less pleased with me. I'm going out with Roberto tonight.'

Janet remained silent, and her very silence proclaimed disapproval.

'I came home to see Luke,' Shelley offered unhappily in explanation. 'I want to spend as much time with him as I can, but I'm not permitted to. Emma guards and restricts his waking hours. I—we had words over it this morning.'

Janet spared her a speculative glance. 'And you expect Mitch to take sides?'

'If he did, it would have to be with Emma.'

'Extra days when there are so few left——'

'I appreciate that,' Shelley intervened wretchedly.

'Emma returns to Cairns tomorrow evening for the weekend,' Janet told her. 'Mary Sutcliffe is quite a different girl—pleasant and very easy to get along with.'

'Thank heaven—another like Emma would be impossible!'

'What time is Roberto calling for you?' Janet queried, adroitly changing the subject as she sliced beef fillets ready for grilling.

'About nine,' Shelley began, and nibbled at a

crisp lettuce leaf. 'We shan't leave until after Luke has gone to bed.'

'Who's "we", young Shelley?' Luke's voice teased from behind. 'And just what is happening after I've gone to my bed?'

'Luke! You've been listening at the door,' she accused laughingly, and went at once to bestow a kiss to his temple.

'Unashamedly,' he revealed laconically.

'Just for that I won't let you cheat at the game of cards we're going to have before dinner,' she chastised teasingly.

'Thought my lucky streak was rather strange,' Luke chuckled, his bright eyes affectionate as they roved over her neat slim figure. The gold dress she was wearing highlighted her ash-blonde hair and accentuated the glowing tan of her skin.

'Huh!'

'After dinner we'll cajole Louise and Mitch into a game of poker—then we'll see if you can still make saucy remarks,' he threatened with a smile.

'One remedy for a saucy woman is to plunge her into the nearest stream,' came a low-pitched laconic drawl, and Shelley turned swiftly to meet Mitch's tawny gaze mere inches away.

'Providing you can catch her first,' she sallied with an impish grin. 'Besides, there's no stream within miles.'

His eyes darkened appreciably and his voice came dangerously soft. 'I'm not beyond improvising, little one.'

'Am I to be hauled over the coals, Mitch?' she asked.

'Not this time,' he answered enigmatically. 'But

perhaps you'll give me a résumé of your plans for the next few days?'

Supremely conscious of Luke's interested gaze, Shelley bit back the retort she longed to make. 'I thought I'd take Lynn and Hal up to Lake Barrine tomorrow, and possibly Cairns on Monday. If that meets with your approval, of course?' she finished sweetly.

'Why not?' he answered calmly. 'We'll take the Range-Rover and make a day of it.'

'We?'

'I'm not so busy that Ken can't be left in charge while I take a day off,' he explained amiably. 'Any objections?'

'None at all. I'm only too happy to have all that driving taken off my hands,' Shelley grinned, and pulled a slight face at him.

Luke began to chuckle and his eyes fairly danced with mischief. 'Darned if you haven't managed to have the last word, young Shelley!'

'Probably the first and final time,' she accorded witchingly.

'It must be the kitchen,' Mitch declared with mock puzzlement. 'Always was a woman's domain.'

'Take him away, Luke,' Shelley begged.

The evening meal seemed to be a continuation of their pre-dinner camaraderie, with witticisms and droll comments flowing effortlessly back and forth across the table. Even Emma forgot herself sufficiently to smile at someone other than Mitch.

Roberto presented himself among their midst a few minutes before nine, and succeeded in creating a ripple of speculation that was evident from Lynn's interested expression and Emma's gleam of satisfaction. Janet was carefully bland, Luke watchful,

91

and there was little to be discerned from Mitch's inscrutable features.

'Would you like to go into town for a few drinks?'

Shelley glanced at Roberto's aquiline profile as he edged the car towards the main road, and was about to reply when he continued speaking.

'Perhaps you would prefer to come to my parents' home?'

'A few drinks in town would be fine,' she acquiesced.

'And coffee afterwards?'

Shelley smiled in the darkness. He really was a very nice man, and if Mitch wasn't the whole entity in her life she could do a lot worse than Roberto Parelli. 'And coffee afterwards, Roberto,' she agreed laughingly.

'Our families have known each other for a long time,' he intimated as they sat at a corner table in the dim recess of the hotel lounge. Shelley elected to sip a shandy in preference to Roberto's Campari.

'The Parellis and the Ballantynes,' she mused thoughtfully. 'Both in their second generation here. No doubt a decade from now there'll be a young son each to take your place.'

'That is life—*si*? To work hard, to gift to your son land that holds sweat from years of toil.'

'What if a son didn't share his father's sentiments?' she couldn't help querying with interest, and Roberto shrugged.

'One shouldn't have children to fashion them to be an extension of oneself.'

'Many do,' Shelley alluded.

'Parental authority—all-encompassing.'

'But that's just the point. It shouldn't be,' she protested earnestly.

Roberto smiled, and his eyes gleamed across the table. 'Shelley Anderson, protector of the young.'

'I left my chalk and lectures back in Brisbane,' she chuckled disarmingly. 'At least, I think I did.'

'You should marry and have children of your own,' he declared gently, and she had to glance away from the warmth in his eyes.

'One day, perhaps,' she answered lightly.

'A man would give much to possess a wife such as you.'

Shelley felt instinctively that she was on shaky ground, and made an attempt to laugh it off. 'I'm not so sure I want to be any man's possession. Certainly not for the redeeming qualities of being domestically efficient, and good with children!'

'I doubt they would be foremost, Shelley,' Roberto assured her wryly as she finished her drink. 'Another?'

'Please.' Anything to swerve away from their present trend of conversation! She watched him walk across the room to the bar, noticing idly that his dark good looks drew more than one girl's attention.

'The barman will think I'm a regular patron—this is the second time I've been in this lounge today,' she imparted when he returned.

'Not alone?' he quirked an eyebrow in mild surprise.

'With Lynn and Hal,' she laughed.

'Ah, yes. Your cousins.'

'Not mine, Roberto.'

'I'm sorry—one tends to forget,' he amended soberly. 'What will you do afterwards, Shelley?'

She looked at him curiously. 'Go back to Brisbane and continue my teaching career. Why?'

'You would not consider staying here?'

She swallowed and attempted to smile. 'I don't see how that's possible.'

'Mitch would not insist that you go,' Roberto essayed with quiet certainty, frowning as she shook her head.

'No. But I have no right to remain,' she explained gently.

'You could marry me.'

Simple words that were sincerely meant, and her tender heart felt for the man seated opposite.

'Roberto——' she began hesitantly, and was surprised to see him smile.

'It's Mitch, isn't it? I've known for some time,' he elaborated quietly. 'I had hoped it might be little more than teenage infatuation, but it is not.'

'What makes you think that?' she asked after a long silence, her eyes wide and pleading.

'I have seen the way you look at him when you've thought no eyes were upon you.'

'I'm sorry,' she whispered.

'Don't be—never be sorry for loving like that,' he returned swiftly.

'Perhaps you'd better take me home,' she suggested miserably.

'Why? Am I such terrible company?'

Shelley saw a smile lurking at the edges of his wide mouth, the hint of sadness in the depths of those dark eyes, and wished with all her heart that it could have been different. 'No,' she smiled shakily.

'Then we shall pretend what has been said between us was never said at all, and we shall enjoy what is left of the evening. *Si?*' he queried, faintly quizzical.

'Yes,' she agreed, adding with sincerity, 'I wouldn't like to lose your friendship, Roberto.'

'It isn't possible for a man and a woman to be friends, Shelley. Always there is an awareness on the part of one, if not the other.'

'You don't want to see me again,' she began sadly.

'Of course I want to see you again,' he argued gently. 'That is the failing of being in love—one never completely gives up.'

Shelley didn't say anything. Perhaps in a few years' time she could come back, but even as the thought chased through her mind she dismissed it. It wouldn't be fair to expect him to accept that he was second-best.

'Come, the hotel is closing. We will walk to the café and have that coffee.'

It appeared quite a few others had the same idea, and they managed to squeeze into a small alcove with another couple, and conversation of necessity was confined to general topics.

'If I were to kiss you, would it be to have you struggle in my arms?'

Roberto's car had only minutes before drawn to a halt on the grass verge several yards at the rear of the homestead. Shelley looked across the brief space between them and shook her head.

It began as a gentle caress, the warmth of his lips touchings hers, the firm pressure of his hands on her shoulders, and it was only when he moved slightly away that she became aware of his quickened breathing.

'It would not take much for me to kiss you differently,' he began intently. 'Perhaps you had better go inside.'

'It was a pleasant evening,' she offered softly. 'Thank you.'

'Will you let me take you out again?'

Slowly she shook her head. 'It wouldn't be fair.'

Roberto reached out a hand and let his fingers trail gently down her cheek. 'If things don't work out with Mitch, I want you to know that I would be prepared to marry you though you don't love me. Perhaps, in time, you could, and for me it would be enough that you were mine.'

'For a while,' Shelley answered quietly. 'Then you would become angry with yourself and with me.'

'I swear to you—*no*.' He smiled a little and touched her lips. 'Not for all can there be a love equal in the fires of passion—a depth of emotion that is part of the soul. Some of us are content with a lesser warmth, and in the end it can be just as satisfying.'

Such profoundness brought tears to her eyes, and they were still there after she bade him goodnight and had entered the house.

Closing the hall switch, she moved towards the kitchen with the intention of getting a glass of iced water from the fridge, and came to an abrupt halt as she saw Mitch sitting at the table with a cup of coffee in his hand.

'It's not that late, is it?' Hesitant words she hadn't meant to utter.

His expression was totally serious as he turned to face her, his dark tawny eyes narrowing fractionally as they fastened on the suspicious shimmer evident in her own.

'The lighter side of midnight, Shelley,' he answered quietly, and when she didn't move he indi-

Postage will
be paid by
Mills & Boon
Limited

Do not affix postage stamps
if posted in Gt. Britain,
Channel Islands or N. Ireland.

BUSINESS REPLY SERVICE
Licence No. CN 81

Mills & Boon Reader Service,
PO Box 236, Thornton Road,
CROYDON, Surrey CR9 9EL.

2

cated the coffee pot near the centre of the table. 'Care to join me?'

At once she was thrown into a flurry of emotions, part of her wanting to accept, another silently urging her to make good her escape.

'I'll get something cool,' she responded tremulously. Oh, what was wrong with her? Quite desperately she wished Janet was present so that she could smile and make light of the past few hours. If Mitch kept watching her so intently she'd do something stupid like bursting into tears.

'Are you going out with him again?' The query was dangerously soft and slightly edged with steel.

Not trusting herself to speak, she shook her head, and became intent with the task of filling a glass with iced water from a jug in the fridge—something which needed her undivided attention if she wasn't to drop and break the glass.

'What time do you want to get away tomorrow?' Shelley asked when the silence between them had stretched interminably. She didn't hear him move, so that when his voice came from close behind she jumped involuntarily.

'Was it so difficult?'

'What—what do you mean?' she stammered as his hands closed on her shoulders.

'You're quivering with nervous reaction and close to tears.' His voice was strangely quiet, and she made no demur as he turned her round to face him.

'It's not often a girl learns she's to inherit a large sum of money, then receives a proposal of marriage all in one day,' she answered shakily, running the tip of her tongue along the lower edge of her lip. 'I don't want it, Mitch.'

His smile was curiously gentle. 'The so-called

inheritance, or the offer of marriage?'

'That's not very funny!'

'Granted. It's a very serious subject,' he acceded lightly.

She raised large eyes to meet his and felt her bones melt at the warmth evident in those tawny depths. 'I wish you every happiness, Mitch.'

His head lowered down to hers and his lips began a gentle exploration across the delicate hollows at the base of her throat, moving to the lobe of her ear and trailing fire over a finely-moulded cheekbone before fastening on her mouth.

There was a wealth of seduction in his touch, and unconsciously her arms crept up around his neck. Almost at once she was drawn close against him and the pressure of his lips increased as she became lost in the warmth of his passion. This was where she belonged, and there seemed no shame in returning his embrace.

When at last she drew back and gently disentangled her arms, she felt bemused and all too aware of her rapid breathing.

'Bed, Shelley,' Mitch determined quietly.

Without hesitation she fled, and once in her room she sank down on to the counterpane to put trembling hands to her burning cheeks as realisation dawned. The memory of those kisses and how they kindled unknown fires deep within made her bite her lip in anguish. Slowly she made ready for bed and slipped between the cool sheets to toss and turn restlessly for ages before falling into an uneasy sleep.

As Mitch wanted to be back by mid-afternoon, they made an early start the following morning, getting on the road shortly after eight o'clock.

There was scarcely a cloud in the azure sky and the surrounding bush-covered hills provided a dark green background for the acres of fresh green cane. The heat of the sun was not at its zenith and there was a freshness in the air that became more apparent as the Range-Rover cruised over the back road to Mareeba, climbing through Mount Molloy and Biboohra and the mountains that formed part of the Great Divide. To have followed the Captain Cook highway along the coast and then climbed the Kuranda Ranges would have added several miles to their journey, and while the latter held possibly more scenic interest, time was of the essence.

At Biboohra there emerged evidence of tobacco farms with acres of rich sandy-loamed soil laid bare and meticulously harrowed in preparation for the new season's young plants. As they drew nearer to Mareeba, tractors towing planting machines could be seen in many paddocks, while in others young plants were firmly established and rose two feet high from the ground.

Passing through Mareeba township with its modern hotels and shops mingling with those of sun-drenched wooden structures well aged with the passing years, one became aware of the bustling activity as farmers brought their wives to replenish weekly-bought provisions. At this time of year when the tobacco season was barely under way it was customary to spend most of Friday in town, giving the men time to yarn companionably over a beer in the bar of either one of three hotels while their women-folk took the opportunity of pleasantly gossiping between shops.

Under Mitch's firm hands the vehicle gathered

speed as it moved along the Kennedy Highway towards Tolga where they would continue to Tinaroo Falls Dam.

Shelley knew this route like the back of her hand, having travelled it countless times during her sojourn at boarding school. Soon the tobacco-growing industry would be left behind, giving way to peanut farming and dairying, and without the soft green paddocks of young tobacco to relieve the almost desert-red sandy soil, the land took on a drier, more arid appearance that would gain little relief until the wet season shed rain unceasingly for several weeks on end, and only then would there be fresh green re-growth to soften the landscape. Of necessity, farmers had to irrigate their crops, and from the air a patchwork of green paddocks and dry red soil provided a startling panorama.

Tinaroo Falls Dam was a tourist spectacle, harnessing as it did such a vast quantity of water, with spray rising high above the falling deluge as it crashed below the spillway. Although sounding suspiciously of Aboriginal origin, it was not, and local conjecture accredited the name to the fact that tin was discovered in this locality and a shout of 'Tin! Haroo!' by the jubilant discoverer led to the area assuming the place-name it bore today.

Lynn was in her element, sketching rapidly as Mitch and Hal opened cans of beer as a means of liquid refreshment, while Shelley elected to dilute hers with lemonade. Several of the scones from a batch made before breakfast disappeared in quick succession, and Mitch foraged in the picnic hamper for the inevitable slice of cake or iced biscuit to round off their early smoko.

Lynn abstractedly selected a scone just as Shelley

was about to pack the hamper, and only when they became mobile and had passed through Kairi en route to Atherton did she reach into the portable chilly-bin for a can of lemonade. The several sketches she had made obviously held most of her attention, and it wasn't until they were a few miles east of Atherton that she joined in the conversation.

A swim in the cool water was opted for unanimously almost as soon as the Range-Rover came to a halt in the parking area of the reserve encroaching Lake Barrine, and Shelley urged Lynn towards the changing rooms.

'Hurry up, do,' she bade them engagingly as they both shed clothes and donned bikinis. Hers was a deep jade green that showed her tanned limbs to advantage, and Lynn cast an admiring glance.

'I look a pale lily in comparison,' she evinced enviously, and Shelley gave a self-effacing grin.

'It's impossible not to acquire a tan in the tropical north. Come on, Lynn,' she urged. 'If we don't get into the water first, we won't have much choice as to the how or where of it—not if I know Mitch!'

They emerged first by a mere few seconds, and Shelley broke into a run and tossed a wicked grin over one shoulder as Mitch sprinted after them.

The water was heavenly, and after a few leisurely strokes Shelley was content to watch Lynn splash her brother unmercifully before he had a chance to enter the lake. Retaliation ensued, and in no time at all Hal caught up and rendered a thorough ducking.

Shelley began to laugh at their antics and didn't notice Mitch disappear as he slipped effortlessly underwater towards her. The first she knew of his presence was when she heard him surface directly behind her, and by then it was too late to take evasive action.

Her revenge was sweet, as almost half an hour later when he was least expecting it she carefully chose her moment and pulled him under. She should have foreseen what would happen next and been prepared for it, but she wasn't, and just as a triumphant laugh escaped her lips hard hands caught about her waist and she was dragged beneath the surface to come up seconds later spluttering and frankly indignant.

Mitch spread his hands high in a mocking gesture of self-defence as he tread water, and his teasing—'Only fish open their mouths under water, little one'—merely served to increase her exasperation.

Shaking water and wet hair from her face she shook a threatening fist at him. 'Just you wait, Mitchell Ballantyne!'

'Not for much longer,' he returned cryptically.

'Meaning—you'll let me duck you?' she sallied in open amazement.

'Ah, now for that you'll have to exert brute force.' His eyes gleamed tantalisingly. 'Out of the water, my girl. It's nearly time for lunch.'

'I am not your girl!'

His mouth curved into a gentle smile as he reached out and tucked a tendril of wet hair back behind her ear, then queried softly, 'Aren't you?'

'There's too much competition,' she quipped lightly, trying to ignore the curling sensation deep in her stomach as she began swimming towards the lake's edge.

Towelled dry, her wet hair combed into a semblance of order, and with a short sleeveless jacket over her bikini, Shelley unpacked the picnic hamper on to the rug spread out on the grass a short distance from the Range-Rover. Cold chicken, lettuce, tomatoes, and hard-boiled eggs reposed in plastic containers and there were buttered rolls, numerous slices of cooked beef as well as cheese and thick wedges of fruit cake.

After such a feast no one felt inclined to swim, and while Mitch and Hal each selected a can of beer Shelley poured coffee out of a Thermos for herself and Lynn.

'It's peaceful here,' Lynn commented as she glanced around the reserve.

'It's a different proposition in the height of summer,' Mitch enlightened, taking cigarettes and matches from his shirt pocket. He had shed his swimming trunks for hip-hugging denim jeans over which he wore a shirt left casually unbuttoned with the lower front edges tied in a knot at his waist.

'The winterless North,' Hal contributed with a lazy gleam, and Shelley laughed.

'Don't forget the Wet,' she reminded him. 'It rains practically non-stop for weeks on end, and all the creeks become raging torrents, some flooding the road in low-lying areas. And it's hot and damp, and tempers become frayed with little provocation,' she added impishly, seeing his grimace of distaste.

'Spare me! I'll stick to the lower half of the continent—the more civilised half.'

'No spirit of adventure,' Lyn declared. 'Give me the wide open spaces any time.'

'Crocodile hunts, country race meetings—and I mean country,' Shelley enthused. 'No recognised track, just a clear stretch of ground in the middle of nowhere.'

'Dirt, dust and flies,' Mitch attested tolerantly.

'And a willy-willy that springs up from nowhere,' Shelley added, describing a whirlwind of dust.

'Don't forget the snakes,' Lynn grinned, unabashed.

'Or the goannas.'

'Ugh!' Shelley shuddered, and glanced reprovingly at Mitch, who merely smiled back broadly.

'Did you have a brush with a goanna, Shelley?' Lynn asked curiously.

'Not exactly——'

'—merely happened unexpectedly upon one,' Mitch continued quizzically as Shelley pulled a face at him.

'What did you do?' Lynn queried as he began to laugh.

'Gave an almighty yell that had every insect and animal scattering for miles around.'

'And stood rooted to the spot?'

'No—she turned tail and ran straight into a tree,' Mitch related without a trace of humour.

'I saw stars, and gave everyone an anxious few days,' Shelley imparted ruefully, glancing across at him. 'That particular trip was ill-fated, wasn't it?'

'When?' Hal asked languidly.

'Four years ago. Luke and I took Shelley outback to Alice Springs and Ayers Rock.'

'Camping?'

'In the Range-Rover, stopping each night to pitch tent and cook a meal over a camp-fire,' Shelley mused dreamily. 'It was great, apart from a little gremlin that dogged my footsteps.'

'What else happened, for heaven's sake?'

'We had to rush Shelley into hospital at Alice

Springs for an emergency appendectomy,' Mitch relayed wryly.

'Some gremlin!' Lynn exclaimed.

'I'm going for a walk,' Shelley determined as soon as she had repacked the picnic hamper. 'Want to come, Lynn?'

'I'll get my pad—I want a good vantage point to sketch the lake.'

They wandered out of sight together, and when Lynn found a spot to her liking Shelley walked on alone round the curve, enjoying the solitude.

Lake Barrine was a crater lake, its name being connected with a local legend, and it was a popular place for picnics and swimming. Shelley wandered on a short way, then sat down and gazed across the surface of the lake. Lynn was right, she mused idly. It was peaceful here—all the more so for being able to escape Mitch's disturbing presence for a while.

'So this is where you've got to.'

Shelley looked up at the sound of that droll cynical voice and tried to hide her annoyance.

'Where's Mitch?' she questioned baldly, and saw Hal's eyes narrow slightly.

'My mechanically-minded cousin has his head buried beneath the bonnet of the Range-Rover.'

'We should get back,' she stated wearily as she stood to her feet. 'No doubt he'll want to get away soon.'

'Plenty of time.' Hal moved towards her, and Shelley immediately took a backward step. 'Oh, come on—what harm is there in a kiss or two?'

'No harm at all if the desire is mutual,' she said evenly, turning away from him.

'Don't walk away from me,' he gritted, and he swung her round with a violence that almost unbalanced her. 'Regular little iceberg, aren't you?'

'Can't you take your frustrations out on someone else?' Shelley queried coldly.

'I'm a red-blooded male, honey,' Hal retorted wryly, his expression hardening as he caught the look of distaste in her face.

'Go and find some other female to amuse yourself with,' she dismissed wearily, making an effort to free herself from his grasp.

'Why should I when there's one right in front of me?'

'If you don't let my arm go——'

'You'll do what?' he queried mockingly, jerking her taut body close, and his eyes glittered hatefully as he lowered his face down to hers. 'Come on, little girl. Fight me—if you can!'

Shelley met his eyes calmly. 'I'll hurt you, Hal,' she said quietly. 'I can, you know, and I won't hesitate if you don't let me go right this minute.'

His eyes narrowed fractionally. 'A tiny slip of a thing like you?'

'What I have in mind doesn't require bodily strength,' she assured him distinctly, then gave a gasp of pain as his fingers dug viciously into her flesh.

'What other tricks has my arrogant cousin taught his little ewe lamb, eh? He's no monk, sweetheart— but perhaps you know that already?'

'Your mind needs fumigating.'

'Oh, come now—have I shocked your sensibilities by suggesting your hero has feet of clay?' he mocked cynically.

'Go and take a cold shower, Hal,' she advised evenly.

'Cool little bitch, aren't you?'

'I'm sweet and adorable, too.' She tilted her head a little and forced a wide smile to her lips. If he thought she was amused he might leave her alone— she hoped! Honestly, he was the most egotistical, thoroughly objectionable man she'd ever had the misfortune to encounter!

'Who are you saving yourself for?' he asked derisively. 'Few men want to waste time with a timid beginner.'

Shelley managed a light laugh. 'That's a rather hackneyed phrase, Hal, and solely a persuasive ploy. Can't you come up with something more original?'

'You really are cool, aren't you? I wonder what it would take to make you beg for mercy?' he gibed sardonically, and caught hold of a length of her hair.

She winced as he gave it a sharp tug, and made one last effort. 'Your tactics are distinctly juvenile— I've known six-year-olds who could devise a——' an anguished gasp escaped her lips and tears sprang to her eyes at the sudden pain he inflicted. Without hesitation she kicked him sharply, the heel of her sandal connecting painfully with his shin.

'Bitch!' He thrust her away with a force that made her stumble back several steps before managing to regain her balance. 'How I'd like to——'

'I wouldn't advise it,' an icily-pitched drawl intruded, and Shelley's eyes flew to the tall rugged frame not far distant.

'Hark the gallant knight!' Hal announced with a bitter laugh. 'No cause for alarm, cousin—your chaste maiden is quite untouched.'

'No thanks to you, I gather,' Mitch accorded silkily, and Shelley suppressed an involuntary shiver at the cold hard anger beneath the surface of his control.

'I never could resist a pretty girl,' Hal shrugged, and Mitch's eyes hardened measurably as they raked glittering ice from Hal's feet slowly upwards to halt at eye-level.

'Resist this one,' he advised softly. 'I can promise a broken jaw if you so much as come within touching distance,' he concluded with dangerous asperity.

'Like that, is it?' Hal managed a cursory lift of his shoulders and began to move away with an exaggerated casual gait.

Shelley smoothed a shaky hand through the length of her hair. The past few minutes had been highly emotive—explosive, she amended unsteadily. It might never have happened if she hadn't chosen to take a solitary walk.

Mitch cast her a look that was deep and unfathomable, and after a few seconds she glanced away. The desire to fling herself into those strong arms and have them close protectively about her was almost more than she could bear.

'Your obnoxious cousin isn't the first man whose unwelcome attentions I've had to fend off!' She drew a deep ragged breath, blind anger forcing her to continue. 'I'm all grown up, Mitchell Ballantyne —or hadn't you noticed?'

'The mere thought has been keeping me awake nights,' he essayed wryly, and she raised startled eyes to meet his, searching for something she daren't define in those tawny depths.

It seemed like a moment out of time, and she had the strange sensation that if she tried to speak her voice would let her down. Almost in slow motion she watched as he reached out and cupped her face between his hands, and the gentle caress of his lips on hers turned her bones to jelly. Then without a word he released his hold and circled an arm round her shoulders as he led her back along the path.

As they rounded the bend and came within sight of the Range-Rover Shelley broke away. 'I'll go and fetch Lynn,' she choked desperately, and all but ran across the grass to the clumps of trees Lynn was busily sketching.

'Time to leave? I've just about finished,' Lynn declared, stroking her pencil rapidly over the pad. 'You seem a bit agitated. Who's responsible—the indubitable Mitch, or that boorish brother of mine?'

'Both!' Shelley vouchsafed succinctly.

'Maddening creatures, men,' Lynn chuckled wryly, pursing her lips as she glanced down at her pad.

'I think I'll remain a career girl, dedicated to my profession,' Shelley managed lightly, and her eyes widened at the sudden perceptive look Lynn gave her.

'I think that's most unlikely.'

'What makes you say that?'

'You're far too nice to remain single for long,' Lynn imparted dryly. 'What's more, you're so darned attractive it isn't quite fair! Ordinary types like me fade into obscurity—I declare that dashing Italian never even noticed I was in the same room!'

'Roberto?' Shelley queried speculatively, and caught Lynn's amused nod. 'He's a likeable man.'

'Stunning,' the other girl corrected with emphasis, causing Shelley to smile.

'He's all yours—I'll even wish you the best of luck.'

'I think the sun has suddenly become brighter,' Lynn declared impudently, and placed her arm through Shelley's as they began walking back towards the Range-Rover.

The homeward drive didn't seem to take as long, although Mitch was unusually quiet, almost withdrawn, and Hal sat sprawled in the front seat with a morose expression on his face, not deigning to offer much by the way of conversation.

More than once Shelley was aware of the penetrating glance Mitch spared her via the rear-vision mirror. Darn him—she'd jolly well close her eyes and pretend to doze! Lynn was caught up with the passing scenery and no doubt was pondering her chances with Roberto. It was quite obvious an attempt at scintillating conversation would be wasted effort!

Within ten minutes of arriving home Mitch downed a quick cup of tea that Janet had ready in the kitchen, then he disappeared out into the paddock. Lynn and Hal declared the need for a shower, a change of clothes, and a rest before dinner.

'This is the worst part of going on a picnic,' Shelley pulled an expressive face at the hamper Mitch had deposited on the floor close to the sink.

'Never mind,' Janet soothed. 'Dinner is all prepared—a little earlier than usual tonight as Mitch will want to leave about seven to drive Emma down to Cairns. If we clear this lot up now, you'll have time for a shower and be able to wash your hair before Luke comes out from his room.'

Mitch was his usual relaxed self over dinner, and Emma appeared to relax her guard somewhat—no doubt due to the fact that she would have Mitch all to herself for an hour in a very short time, Shelley thought uncharitably. Possibly longer if the girl was successful in angling an invitation for the remainder of the evening.

There was a familiar surge of jealousy as she casually wished Emma a polite goodbye, and the sight of the girl sitting beside Mitch in the front seat of the Chrysler heralded a momentary flaring of terrible rage that took all her self-discipline to control!

With determined effort she suggested a game of cards to while away an hour until it was time for Luke's favourite television programme to begin.

'Come and play for me, Shelley,' Luke bade around nine o'clock when Hal offered to assist him into bed.

'Half an hour,' Shelley warned gently as she sat down on a chair between his bed and the door on to the verandah.

Luke's face creased into the semblance of an impish grin. 'Wouldn't go down well with Emma, would it? She's not here, young Shelley, and while the cat's away the mice can play.'

She began to laugh and her eyes sparkled with mirth. 'You're incorrigible, do you know that?'

'Why should I be anything else?' he queried complacently.

'Like father, like son,' she declared dryly, and he chuckled.

'Play "Country Road", Shelley. I feel like being soothed into melancholic slumber.'

Her fingers began moving softly across the strings, and after a few seconds the words found voice.

'Beautiful,' Luke proclaimed gently when she came to the end of the Denver melody.

'Yes.'

Shelley turned swiftly at the sound of that low-

111

pitched drawl and felt the butterflies begin their familiar tattoo somewhere in the region of her stomach at the sight of Mitch leaning negligently against the door frame.

'You're back,' she said unnecessarily.

He smiled as he straightened and moved slowly to stand behind her chair. 'You sound surprised, little one. Weren't you expecting me to come back?'

Thoroughly cross, she turned away and immediately felt his hands resting lightly on her shoulders.

'Ah,' he teased musingly. 'But not so quickly, hmm?'

Her smoky eyes implored Luke to say something, but he ignored her silent appeal and eyed them both with an almost waiting expectancy.

'I'll go back to the lounge.' Cool calm words that belied her emotions.

'Not yet,' Mitch advocated softly, his hands curling about her shoulders exerting just sufficient pressure to enforce his words.

Why—why was he behaving like this? she puzzled helplessly, then almost died as she felt his lips brush against her hair.

'We'll break open the champagne tomorrow,' he declared with quiet significance. 'When Luke can join us in a toast. But I think we owe it to him to be the first to know.'

Know what? she almost cried out aloud.

'I've seen it coming for a long time,' Luke said gently. 'Shelley is very much her mother's daughter.'

'Totally irresistible,' Mitch affirmed indulgently.

Shelley glanced at Luke with desperation, met the happy contentment in his eyes, and didn't have the heart to utter any words in denial.

'I hoped, I prayed,' he assured her quietly. 'There

were times when I chided myself for being a foolish old man,' he finished gently, and there were tears of happiness in his eyes.

Oh, Mitch, she cried silently. Why—how could you do this to him—to *me*?

'I intend to see that she doesn't regret one minute of it,' Mitch vowed softly, then to Shelley's utter consternation he pulled her to her feet and kissed her thoroughly. Releasing his hold, he gently led her the short distance to Luke's side, and with an inarticulate sound she bent down to let him kiss her cheek.

'Tears, Shelley?'

She looked down into his kindly face, and the suspicious shimmer in her eyes became a slow-trickling flow down each cheek. The hand that brushed them away was trembling and so were her lips as she forced them into a semblance of a smile. 'We females are a contrary lot,' she managed shakily.

'I think a stroll in the garden is indicated,' Mitch drawled musingly.

'Definitely!' Luke's laughing eyes met those of his son and he chuckled. 'Best place for the kind of reassurance you have in mind.'

'I can think of a better one,' Mitch declared with lazy mockery as he drew Shelley into the curve of his arm and held her firmly against him. 'But that will have to wait.' He slanted a smile down towards her head that rapidly widened into a wicked grin as she resolutely refused to lift her gaze from the region of Luke's bed. 'Dear Shelley,' he teased gently, 'I do believe you're blushing.'

Well, two can play at that game, she determined fiercely as slow anger began to replace bemusement. Summoning all her reserves of strength, she lifted

113

her head and cast him a bewitching smile—only her eyes weren't smiling, they were agleam with fury.

'Luke needs his sleep, darling,' she chastised gently, and the *darling* nearly choked her. 'It's well past his bedtime.'

'Yes, go—both of you,' Luke bade easily, smiling as Shelley leant down and bestowed a kiss at his temple.

Almost as soon as they were down the steps Shelley attempted to free herself from the strength of that encircling arm, only to have it tighten measurably, and his dangerously soft—'not yet'—stilled any further struggles until they had walked a considerable distance from the house.

'How could you?' burst from her lips in a furious whisper just as soon as they reached the edge of the side paddock.

'Precisely how could I—what?' Mitch countered with maddeningly imperturbability.

'Let Luke think that you and I—that we——' she faltered indignantly, and was further infuriated when he voiced with mild interest:

'Yes, Shelley?'

'Why did you imply that we might become engaged?' she bit out angrily, trying to wrench away from him with little success.

'I was under the impression I more than implied it,' he answered quietly. 'Tomorrow the rest of the household will be told.'

She could only gaze at him speechlessly, then returning sanity prevailed. 'The engagement is to be a pretence for Luke's benefit.'

'No pretence, little one,' he evinced dryly. 'I have no intention of deceiving Luke over something which means so very much to him.'

'You could have asked me first,' she flung help-lessly, at a loss to understand him.

'And give you time to think up any number of reasons why you should refuse?' he queried wryly.

'Why me, Mitch?' she asked heatedly. 'And why now? Is your conscience bothering you over what to do with me after Luke dies—is that it?'

That she had gone too far was evident as the pressure of his hands on her arms increased to an excruciating level of pain. 'Mitch—*please!*' she begged in a strangled whisper. 'I'm sorry.'

'Go back inside the house, Shelley.' His voice was formidably bleak. 'Before I do something regrettable.'

Without a word she slipped out of his grasp and turned towards the house, tears blinding her vision as she broke into a stumbling run. She had gone only a few yards when her foot struck something hard on the ground, and she stumbled down on to her hands and knees. With a muffled sob she scrambled to her feet and began to run just as hard hands grasped her shoulders.

'Let me go!' Shelley cried brokenly, struggling hopelessly against him.

'I've no intention of letting you go,' Mitch declared with ominous asperity. 'Be still, child!'

His command had effect and she stood silently, not able to look at him.

'Are you hurt?'

*Yes,* she longed to cry. I hurt deep inside—so much so that it's almost a physical ache. But she shook her head mutely and refused to meet his gaze. Her hand must have grazed against one of the rocks bordering the garden, for it had begun to throb painfully and she could feel something warm and sticky trickling down her wrist to mingle with a quantity of soil clinging to her fingers.

'Nevertheless, I'll check,' he determined quietly, and led her through the gardens towards the side steps on to the verandah near the study. The door shut behind them and he switched on the light, giving her little chance to escape.

Shelley looked straight ahead at the material of his shirt, and sensing his raking scrutiny she held her injured hand firmly behind her.

'Your hands, Shelley. Let me see them,' he bade with deceptive calm, and when she didn't move he reached out and brought them forward.

She gazed in fascination at the large graze on the fleshy part of her palm just beneath the thumb and saw that the graze extended across her wrist and several inches up her arm. It hurt abominably, and would undoubtedly hurt even more while it was bathed and dressed.

Mitch vented a barely muffled oath in exasperation, then without a word he led her unceremoniously towards the bathroom and proceeded to bathe her hand, changing the water several times before adding disinfectant.

'The sooner I'm in a position to do something about all this pent-up emotion of yours, the better,' he commented wryly as he fixed the gauze bandage in place, and Shelley swallowed the lump that suddenly rose in her throat.

'That's not likely to happen,' she muttered indistinctly as he refilled the basin with clean water, and she ventured a quick look at him from beneath long-fringed lashes.

'No? I'd say it's inevitable,' he replied grimly,

and there was latent savagery in the depths of those tawny eyes.

She stood completely still as he sponged the tear-streaks from her cheeks, for one glance at that taut profile was sufficient for her to stifle any protest she might have made.

'You need some warm milk with a measure of brandy, and perhaps two Paracetamol,' he observed quietly. 'Go and get into bed and I'll bring them in to you.'

Her eyes felt incredibly large as they met his steady gaze, and without demur she moved across the hall to her room, undressing with undue haste in case he should come in before she was safely between the sheets. She made it with only a minute to spare, and when he moved leisurely across to the bed she took the glass and the tablets from his outstretched hand.

Judging from the potency of her drink there was just as much brandy as there was milk. At this rate she'd probably suffer a hangover in the morning!

'I feel like a child again—fed warm milk and tucked into bed by a doting——' she hesitated bemusedly, not feeling herself at all. Perhaps this was a dream from which she would wake and find the events of the past few hours had been the result of her subconscious mind.

A slight smile curved his lips, and the gleam in his eyes was frankly teasing. 'Perhaps I'd better complete that nursery scene,' he drawled as he bent over, and his mouth descended on hers with a lingering sweetness.

'Goodnight, dear Mitch,' she murmured sleepily

as he straightened. 'Thank you for playing nurse-maid.'

'Sleep well, princess,' he commanded softly, then moved out the door and closed it gently behind him.

## CHAPTER SIX

SHELLEY didn't have long to wonder just how and when the rest of the household would be acquainted with news of her engagement to Mitch. Immediately before lunch when everyone, including Ken Pemberton, had gathered out on the verandah for a cool drink Luke took it upon himself to impart the news.

Janet was delighted, her broad smile indicating it to be confirmation of something she had known all along. Louise nodded her head sagely and added her felicitations, whereas Lynn hugged them both ecstatically and declared it couldn't happen to two nicer people. Hal proffered a rather droll congratulationary spiel that made Ken's eyebrows almost disappear into the furrow of his brow, and it said much when Ken stooped to plant a shy kiss on her cheek before slapping Mitch on the shoulder.

There was a further surprise in store when Mitch produced a jewellery box and without further ado slipped a ring on to her finger. And what a ring! Shelley couldn't help the startled gasp that escaped from her lips as she saw the exquisite craftsmanship of the setting and the size of the stones. Two large diamonds set high, with smaller diamonds on the supporting platinum shoulders tracing a delicate arrowhead to the wide gold band that circled her finger.

'It's beautiful,' she could only whisper, and the smile on her lips felt decidedly wobbly.

'Tears, Shelley' Mitch slanted quizzically. 'I can see I'll have no less than a flood to contend with on our wedding day.'

'Which will take place when?' Louise broke in briskly, always one to demand facts.

'Soon,' Mitch allowed easily as Shelley offered a slightly strangled——

'It's not definite yet.'

'Next week,' Luke declared with a determined twinkle in his eye.

'Can it be arranged so quickly?' Louise queried doubtfully, and Hal cast Shelley a look that was entirely speculative.

'That's one advantage of having money, Mother dear,' Lynn offered laughingly. 'It has a way of smoothing the "can't be done" phrase right out of existence!'

'A small family wedding performed here in the gardens,' Luke stated positively. 'And I shall give Shelley away.'

'With Ken as best man, and Lynn the bridesmaid,' Mitch declared, blithely ignoring the despairing look Shelley flung in his direction.

It was all whirling way out of control—someone had to put a stop to it. 'Mitch——' But he seemed oblivious to her beseeching whisper, or was deliberately ignoring it—she wasn't sure which! He appeared to have slipped into the role of a contented loving fiancé, she thought a trifle hysterically as she sipped the champagne that had been speedily produced.

'Did you cut your hand?'

She cast desperate eyes towards Ken as he moved over to stand beside her, and made an effort to appear gay and sparkling. 'Oh, I fell and grazed it on one of the rocks in the garden,' she answered lightly, endeavouring to meet his penetrating gaze.

'Bad luck,' came his sympathetic reply, immediately followed by a slow smile. 'You don't need me to tell you how pleased I am about all this.' He swept an arm to indicate Mitch and herself.

'Thanks, Ken.'

He remained standing there as Lynn came closer with a happy grin creasing her mobile features.

'No doubt about the Ballantynes—when they organise something, they really organise!' She laughed at Shelley's bewildered expression. 'Shelley, you surely didn't imagine my dynamic cousin would observe convention and concede to anything approaching a lengthy engagement?' she queried impishly. 'Mother will be in her element!'

'I didn't expect it to be quite so soon,' Shelley managed shakily, and her heart gave an appreciable lurch as Mitch placed a casual arm around her shoulders. His steady gaze wreaked havoc with her breathing, and he smiled thoughtfully as he caught Lynn's attention.

'I think we'll need a day in Cairns on Monday—shopping,' he elaborated quizzically. 'Louise and Janet can go down with Ken the following day.'

'Wedding finery,' Lynn deduced gaily. 'Shelley and I are going to have quite a weekend deciding colour and style!'

Luke overheard her and interrupted their conversation. 'Choose whatever you want for yourself, but Shelley is wearing something long, white and definitely bridal,' he declared firmly, daring anyone to argue with him.

'Much as I'd like to continue drinking champagne, there is lunch to see to,' Janet declared prosaically, and Shelley grasped the opportunity to escape like a drowning man clutches at a lifeline.

'I'll come with you,' she determined, blandly ignoring Janet's slight look of puzzlement.

The meal passed in a haze of chatter entirely centred around the wedding, its proposed time, the food—and such things as which day it would take place, or more importantly whether the minister would be free to perform the ceremony, were given only a cursory consideration.

Quite desperately she needed to talk to Mitch—although what good it would do she couldn't fathom. He had driven into Mossman on some errand and wouldn't be back until just before dinner.

Luke retired gracefully to his room with little insistence from Mary Sutcliffe, Emma's weekend replacement, and Louise closeted herself in the kitchen with Janet to discuss menu alternatives for the wedding. Lynn managed to gather together several fashion magazines and eagerly led Shelley into the lounge.

'You sort through these while I take this pile,' Lynn commanded engagingly, and began turning pages at random, referring every few minutes for Shelley's opinion.

'Oh, Lynn,' Shelley sighed silently. 'I'm about as emotionally geared for this marriage as that model you're wrapped up in—and I'll have to smile and adopt a radiant façade for Luke's benefit. And afterwards, when it's all over—what then?' An engagement she was agreeable to—she would have pretended for Luke's benefit—but now? Marriage was binding, and not to be lightly undertaken. What on earth was Mitch thinking of, letting it snowball like this? Unless ... No, it was impossible.

'Shelley, you're miles away,' Lynn chided with exasperation. 'Anyone would think you don't care what your bridesmaid wears.'

Shelley pulled her thoughts together with conscious effort and thrust herself with apparent whole-heartedness into the matter at hand. Two hours later they had agreed on blue for the colour of Lynn's dress and accessories, decided on two alternative designs, and discussed bouquets and head-gear. Only Shelley's dress wasn't touched upon—it was to be a surprise, and no one was going to choose it for her! It would be long and white, and definitely bridal as Luke wanted, but she alone was going to decide the style.

During afternoon smoko Shelley's ring was examined and declared quite something.

'Expensive,' Louise murmured, and one could almost see she was calculating its cost. It never ceased to rankle her that her brother had by dint of hard work and good fortune amassed considerable wealth—not that she begrudged him, for it was wishful thinking that her own departed husband hadn't made as much of his opportunities.

'Of course it was the obvious thing to happen,' Louise continued briskly. 'Mitch deciding to marry you,' she elaborated as she encountered Shelley's startled expression. 'Yes, much the sensible thing to do. After all, Luke, fond of you as he is, didn't legally adopt you when he married Cathie. It would have been difficult for you to continue regarding this as your home after he died.'

Janet uttered a brief exclamation that sounded suspiciously like an oath. 'Nonsense! I've seen this marriage coming for years—anyone with half an eye can see Shelley and Mitch are meant for each other.'

Louise selected another cake from the plate and ate most of it before rationalising, 'Perhaps. But you can't deny Luke's condition has precipitated things.'

'Rubbish!' Janet declared adamantly.

This was too much for Shelley, and draining her glass of fruit juice she stood to her feet. 'I have to see Ken about something.' It was a downright fabrication, but she was past caring.

'Ah, yes—the cake,' Janet flew loyally to her rescue, managing to produce as if by magic a cake-tin with an assortment of freshly baked iced squares. 'Don't hurry back, it's only cold meat and a salad for dinner, and if I need any help, Louise or Lynn can give it.'

Without a backward glance Shelley made good her escape, and almost ran all the way down the grassed track to Ken's small cottage.

He, bless him, took little notice of her flustered state and asked no questions, simply poured another cup of tea and waved her into a chair.

'Want to talk about it, Shelley?' he queried matter-of-factly some few minutes later when she failed to offer anything by way of conversation.

She shot him a rueful glance. 'You're the only sane sensible one here,' she declared obliquely.

'Bad as that?'

'Let's just say the attention has swung from Luke to me.'

He took time in answering. 'A wedding is an important event.'

'If it's important to the two people concerned,' she answered quickly.

'And isn't it?'

'Yes—no. Who knows?' she flung desperately.

'I've known Mitch since he was a lad,' Ken commented bluntly. 'Never got into anything he wanted to escape from.'

'It's to please Luke—I know it.'

'No sense in that argument,' he dismissed easily.

'Then why?'

'I would say the usual reason, young Shelley,' he smiled crookedly as he took the makings for a home-rolled cigarette from his pocket.

'He hasn't said so.'

'Must be difficult with a house full of people, one of them a stranger,' he alluded gently, 'and Luke as ill as he is. Perhaps he's taken the only possible course.'

'A girl likes to be asked,' she protested.

'There's little difference when either method leads to the same conclusion.'

'I'm not convinced, Ken.'

'I'll lay you odds,' he grinned amiably, and she pulled a face at him.

'You're pretty safe. If I create a fuss it will break Luke's heart in more ways than one.'

'I wasn't talking about the marriage ceremony,' Ken stated carefully.

'I think you're wrong,' she said slowly, pushing any thoughts of *after* the wedding to the back of her mind. It was enough that she could get through each day, let alone ponder what would happen when she became Mrs Mitchell Ballantyne!

'Time alone will tell.'

Shelley looked at him steadily, then moved her glance around the bachelor kitchen. She felt reluctant to go back to the house just yet, and as Luke had retired later than usual for his siesta it was unlikely he would be out from his room much before dinner. 'What would you say to a home-cooked meal that you didn't have to cook yourself?' she asked speculatively.

'Guess I could stand it,' he grinned tolerantly.

'Anything?'

'You want to cook—so cook!' he ordered.

She began to laugh, and some of her cares slipped away as she busied herself taking stock of cupboards and the contents of the refrigerator.

It was almost six o'clock when she left the cottage after dishing up an appetising filet mignon with potatoes, peas and carrots, followed by a crusty apple pie. A slight smile lit her expressive features as she slipped into the house via the side verandah and made her way down to her bedroom. Ken's gleam of satisfaction when he had sat down to the food she had placed on his table was all the thanks she needed.

A hasty shower and a change of clothes took barely ten minutes, and she spared a quick glance at her reflection as she stroked a brush vigorously through her hair. A cream body-shirt beneath a cunningly-cut dress of dull green that flared out below the bodice and swung loosely about her legs looked fresh and cool, and she applied a minimum of make-up before making her way to the kitchen.

It was empty, the salads and serving plates of cold meat reposing beneath covers on the bench ready to be taken into the dining-room, and with a sigh she turned and made her way down the hall.

Her entrance into the lounge brought the focused attention of everyone in the room, and she doubted any one of them guessed the effort it cost her to smile.

'Sorry I'm late. I stayed to cook Ken a meal,' she offered brightly, and smoothed a stray tendril of hair back behind one ear in a purely nervous gesture.

'Lucky Ken,' Hal observed sardonically.

'There were some details we wanted to go over with you,' Louise chided with a frown. 'It will have to be done after dinner.'

Shelley's eyes flew instinctively towards Mitch, and she was unaware of the sudden anguish that appeared in their smoky-blue depths.

'I think they can be left until tomorrow, Louise,' he intervened smoothly, and moved across the room towards Shelley. 'In case of doubt, refer to me.'

'Men have no idea of the planning involved to ensure everything goes smoothly,' Louise said reprovingly. 'Wednesday is only days away.'

Wednesday! Shelley looked up at Mitch blindly, and felt the warning pressure of his hand on her arm.

'There's very little to arrange,' he declared evenly. 'The minister will arrive at four, and the ceremony will be conducted soon after that. There will be no guests to cater for, as there will be only ourselves and Ken, and although I imagine Janet has something more elaborate than our usual evening fare in mind, I don't doubt she'll manage admirably.'

How could he be so calm!

'Now that Shelley is here, we can go in to dinner,' Janet announced pleasantly.

Only Luke managed to throw a little light humour on the matter by directing a wicked grin towards Shelley and Mitch. 'If you don't leave things well alone, Louise, the pair of them will elope in self-defence.'

'There you are, Mother,' Lynn chuckled unrepentantly. 'You've just been done out of a job. You'll have to be content to be a mere spectator in this one.'

To her credit, Louise took it well. 'If my help isn't needed ...' she allowed her voice to trail off expressively, only to have Janet hasten speedily——

'Oh, but it will be,' she sanctioned sweetly. 'I'll need another pair of hands in the kitchen on Wednesday, because I won't let Shelley within cooee of the stove or sink that day.'

Shelley managed to get through the following few hours with admirable calm, although her smile seemed a little cracked around the edges and her sense of humour had long departed for parts unknown! Louise was irrepressible, and the forthcoming wedding with its precluding shopping excursions into Cairns were the sole topic of her conversation. When Mitch returned to the lounge after assisting Luke into bed, Shelley stood to her feet pleading tiredness.

'If you don't mind, I'll follow Luke's example. It's been quite a day,' she concluded with the semblance of a weary smile.

'Sweet dreams, little one,' Mitch bade quizzically.

'What, no moonlight stroll in the gardens? No goodnight kiss?' Hal queried sardonically.

Shelley didn't bother to answer, and simply flung

a slightly scornful look in his direction as she made her way to the door.

Sleep was elusive, despite the fact that she felt genuinely tired, and after an interminable length of time spent tossing and turning she resorted to a relaxing yoga technique, but even that failed. Obviously she was incapable of applying sufficient concentration—oh, why couldn't she *sleep* for heaven's sake!

The niggling pain in her head had developed into a definite ache, and she felt an emotional wreck. Well, there was nothing else for it but to go into the kitchen for a couple of Paracetamol and a glass of water, she decided wearily, suiting thought to action. Her hair felt tousled and she didn't bother to slip her feet into sheepskin mules, just shrugged her arms into the light brunch-coat at the end of her bed.

The house was in darkness as she crept down the hall, and she shut the kitchen door carefully before turning on the light-switch. It took only seconds to locate the tablets she needed, then she crossed to the sink to fill a glass with water. How it happened she never knew, but the next second there was a splintering crash as the glass slipped to the floor.

Oh, now look what she'd done! she cursed vexedly. She cursed even more when a shaft of broken glass pierced her foot as she manoeuvred her way around the mess to collect a brush and dustpan from a nearby cupboard.

'What in the name of heaven are you up to now?'

Shelley turned sideways from her crouched position and cast the owner of that exasperated drawl a decidedly wrathful look.

'I'm not up to anything,' she countered snappishly, returning her attention to the matter at hand. 'I'm *down* clearing the remains of a broken glass.'

'With nothing on your feet, and one cut already,' Mitch observed dryly. 'You seem unusually prone to mishaps of late.'

'It's all your fault!' she flung vexedly as he calmly bent down and took the brush and pan from her hands and finished the task.

'My dear girl, I wasn't even in the room,' he slanted wryly.

'Oh, don't be so——' she halted crossly. 'You know very well what I mean! Announcing to Luke that we're engaged, then just standing by saying *nothing* when everything begins to get out of hand!'

He dispensed with the broken glass, returned the brush and pan to the cupboard, and when she didn't follow his silent indication to sit on a nearby chair so that he could examine her foot he simply grasped hold of her waist and effortlessly deposited her on the edge of the table.

'I was under the impression that an engagement declared an intention to marry,' he murmured with a measure of cynicism.

'Of course it does—but not five days later,' Shelley accused heatedly, her furious gaze resting on his towelling-robed figure. 'Luke is overjoyed, and Louise has everything planned down to the last detail.' He was so close she could have reached out a hand and touched him, and the desire to do so was almost more than she could bear.

'I take that to mean it's not the prospect of marriage to me that bothers you—merely that it's to be so soon?' he queried mockingly, and there was a slight smile playing the edges of his mouth.

'An engagement to make Luke happy I can understand,' she said wretchedly. 'But marriage . . . How can we possibly back out now?'

His tawny eyes darkened and seemed particularly penetrating as they met her furious gaze. 'Neither one of us will back out, Shelley—make no mistake about it.'

'My foot's quite all right,' she choked irrationally, and endeavoured to pull it from his grasp. 'I'm just as capable as you of putting on a Band-aid strip!'

'And you, my little spitfire, are a hair's breadth away from a good old-fashioned spanking!'

'There you go again, treating me like a child,' she sallied resentfully. 'You don't even think to *ask* if I want to marry you. You—you just place me in an intolerable position where I can't refuse, and— and I hate you for it!' Her furious whisper rose to a high crescendo.

'Hate me as much as you like,' he drawled implacably. 'The wedding goes ahead as planned.'

'A marriage is more difficult to discard than an engagement.'

'It isn't my intention to discard either,' he assured her deliberately.

'Why?'

At that bald, incredulous query he straightened his lengthy frame, and suddenly Shelley wished he hadn't. It was difficult to hold an argument with anyone when you had to crane your neck. It gave you less of an advantage.

'I would have thought that was obvious—even to you.' Calm words spoken steadily, but one glimpse into those amber depths revealed a bleak anger second to none.

Despite the warm temperature Shelley shivered.

'I'll get another glass,' she said quietly, and slipped down on to her feet.

'To have with these?' Mitch picked up the tablets she'd placed on the bench and examined them. 'Unable to sleep, or a headache?'

'Both,' she declared succinctly.

'No doubt the cause of which is indirectly attributed to me,' he deduced mockingly.

Shelley grimaced and shot him a brooding look. 'You always did act first and explain later.'

'It's becoming a habit when dealing with you, little one,' he slanted musingly.

'I wish you'd stop calling me that!'

'Why? The top of your head barely reaches my shoulder, and there's quite a lot less of you. I could manage, darling,' he offered quizzically.

Quite deliberately she turned away from that faint teasing smile. 'No.' A monosyllabic denial that in no way revealed her inner turmoil, and she longed to cry out—'Don't call me that—not unless you mean it'. Her head throbbed dully, reminding her of the reason for her midnight sojourn to the kitchen, and swinging back to face him she took the tablets from his hand and swallowed them down with some water.

'We'd better get back to bed,' she said slowly, then blushed a delicate pink as she caught the hidden laughter gleaming in the depths of his eyes.

'That's not a bad suggestion,' he considered tolerantly. 'Many an argument has been settled there.'

'Well, this one won't be!'

'Not tonight.'

'Not *any* night,' Shelley flung incautiously, glancing away as his features creased with lazy mockery.

'No? You surely don't imagine we'll occupy separate rooms?'

She fell silent, the enormity of such a prospect rendered her incapable of coherent speech.

'Go to bed, Shelley,' Mitch drawled wryly after several minutes, and she escaped from the kitchen and his disturbing presence with a speed that brought a slight twisted smile to his lips.

Shelley spent Sunday in a whirl of activity that gave her little time to think of anything other than the tasks at hand. The gardens received meticulous attention from six o'clock in the morning until midday, with only a brief respite for a hurried breakfast, and, ignoring both Louise and Hal's quirked eyebrows, she spent the afternoon replenishing the cake-tins. Janet sagely decided to maintain silence over such zealousness, and made no demur when Shelley manufactured a tidy pile of mending from a cache of linen that was intended to be donated to charity. Head bent over swiftly flying fingers that joined fabric with needle and thread, Shelley spent the evening hours curled at the foot of Luke's chair, and timed her own exit for when Mitch was absent assisting Luke into bed.

Early Monday morning Mary Sutcliffe drove herself back to the local hospital in Mossman, and Mitch left to collect Emma from Cairns.

It didn't take long for news of the engagement and impending marriage to come to Emma's ears, and there was little genuine warmth in her expressed congratulations. The look she cast Shelley was definitely invidious, and it was something of a relief when the nurse left the breakfast table to attend to Luke.

'Give me Mary Sutcliffe any time,' Lynn murmured wryly. 'Emma may be a paragon of the nursing profession, but ...' she trailed off expressively, and changed the subject. 'Hal, why not come with us?'

'Quite simply because I brought a perfectly adequate suit with me,' he dismissed cursorily. 'In any case, I've no desire to traipse city streets all day in this heat when I have no need to.'

Mitch drained his coffee cup and stood to his feet. 'Hurry it up, girls. I want to be back by mid-afternoon, if possible,' he declared briskly.

'There's so much to do,' Lynn bewailed eloquently.

'Whoa!' Shelley intervened sceptically. 'All I'm buying is a wedding dress, shoes, and a few odd things. That shouldn't take too long.'

Lynn looked scandalised. 'You call acquiring a trousseau "a few odd things"?' she queried incredulously. 'You'll need glamorous nighties and at least one lacy peignoir.'

'I won't, you know,' Shelley replied with intended emphasis, not daring to spare a glance at Mitch.

'Don't tell me you sleep in the altogether, Shelley?' Hal asked with idle cynicism.

'Of course she doesn't,' Janet broke in sharply, and shot him a look that would have withered a less hardy-skinned individual.

'Cotton nighties—demure of neckline with lace and a ribbon or two,' Mitch intimated lazily, his eyes agleam with hidden laughter.

'Ah,' Hal responded speculatively, at which Shelley stood to her feet and took her unfinished coffee into the kitchen.

'Leave those, and go and get ready,' Janet bade

133

quietly as she followed Shelley to the sink.

'I've only lipstick to apply and my shoulder-bag to collect,' Shelley said bleakly. 'That won't take more than a minute.'

Janet darted her a perceptive glance. 'Do it first, then come back if you must,' she placated gently.

'You think I'm over-reacting, don't you?' Shelley questioned wryly.

'My dear, every bride is entitled to indulge in pre-wedding nerves,' Janet smiled slightly. 'However, if you intend following yesterday's example from now until Wednesday, you'll wear yourself out, and Mitch deserves a radiant bride.'

'It's snowballing so fast, I haven't time to feel in the least bridal,' Shelley confessed shakily.

'Take each day as it comes, and——' Janet paused momentarily, then hastened on— 'My dear, Luke is getting such a store by this wedding—choose an exquisite gown, for his sake. His time is running out so fast—let it be a truly memorable day.'

Shelley didn't trust herself to answer. She felt like a puppet on a string, entirely at the mercy of circumstances beyond her control.

The Chrysler sedan sped swiftly towards the coast under Mitch's competent hands, and he kept the conversation flowing with adroit ease, making Lynn laugh as he recounted humorous incidents. Shelley decided her best line of defence was attack, and she slipped in a few reminiscences of her own, with the result they reached Cairns in seemingly no time at all.

The morning flew on wings as the two girls searched shop after shop for their purchases, although Shelley had a difficult time persuading Lynn that she intended choosing her own wedding gown alone. She might as well observe some of the conventional traditions surrounding a wedding, she grimaced slightly, and no one, positively no one was going to catch so much as a glimpse of her gown until she wore it on Wednesday afternoon.

There was a mild hassle over her proposed trousseau, and in the end she capitulated by allowing herself to be coerced into acquiring a concoction of nylon and lace that revealed far more than it concealed. The thought of wearing it to entice Mitch, as Lynn had laughingly suggested, was out of the question—she'd put it away in a drawer somewhere and gift it to one of her friends at Christmas!

From Lynn's dedication to detail, the shop assistants could be forgiven for harbouring the illusion that *the* wedding of the year was about to take place. The exact shade of blue for both shoes and dress, gloves, and floppy-brimmed hat in sheer organza—anyone would have thought Lynn the bride, and Shelley the bridesmaid, instead of the other way around!

By lunch-time the rear seat of the sedan was well covered with parcels of all shapes and sizes, and paled into insignificance the few packages Mitch had already deposited there.

The day was a happy one, and Shelley enjoyed every minute of it, despite those moments when she felt inclined to pinch herself to discover if it was a dream or indeed reality. In the warmth of the spring sunshine, with Lynn's sparkling company to shield her against Mitch, it almost became possible to believe that everything about this proposed marriage was right, that Luke's illness had only precipitated what would have become fact.

'Do you girls need anything else?'

Shelley glanced at Lynn, who was in the process of indicating that they did, and laughingly shook her head at Mitch.

'No, we don't,' she said firmly, giving him a dazzling smile.

His tawny eyes twinkled lazily as he regarded them both. 'One "yes", and one "no"—what is a mere male supposed to deduce from that?'

'That the necessities have all been taken care of,' Shelley sparkled. 'If Lynn had her way——'

'Nighties,' Lynn pronounced with cousinly candour. 'She's bought only one.'

'Ah, I see,' Mitch drawled quizzically as he shot Shelley a devilish smile before turning his attention to Lynn. 'I take it that I'm supposed to be beguiled with a selection of feminine fripperies?'

'Of course—it's all part of a bride's trousseau,' Lynn enthused, and Shelley cast him an impudent grin.

'Lynn is an incurable romantic,' she said lightly. 'If I'd heeded her advice, I would have bought at least seven.'

Mitch began to chuckle. 'You've just been over-ruled, Lynn.'

'You mean you agree with her?'

'I agree that my interest won't be wholly taken up with what my wife will wear to bed,' he declared on a teasing note, and his eyes flared sensually alive as he caught the slow tinge of pink that coloured Shelley's cheeks. 'Come, my innocent angel—on your feet,' he ordered gently.

'We're going home?' Lynn asked doubtfully.

'Home,' he answered firmly, and taking hold of Shelley's hand he proceeded to weave his way from the restaurant to the footpath outside.

She allowed herself to be led to the car, and throughout the drive home made an effort to appear the happy, carefree bride-to-be, as surely she should be. Perhaps it was just pre-wedding jitters, as Janet implied, but oh, dear heaven, at this rate she doubted she'd make Wednesday in one piece! She felt as nervous as a cat on hot bricks, and as for poise—that quality had disappeared entirely!

It didn't exactly help matters to discover on arriving home that Louise had inadvertently tripped down the steps and was now nursing a severely sprained ankle. Although perhaps in one way it was a blessing in disguise, Shelley mused as she unpacked her purchases. At least Louise wouldn't be able to stage-manage the wedding to the degree she had no doubt intended! And Janet would be relieved—she regarded the kitchen as her own particular sanctum, having ruled there for so many years, and to be made to feel that it wasn't, even for a short time, was inclined to make her rather short-tempered!

Luke described it perfectly in an aside to Shelley after dinner that evening.

'That'll have taken the wind out of Louise's sails,' he intimated with quiet humour. 'D'you think I should offer her the use of my wheelchair?' His brown eyes twinkled devilishly up at her.

'I wouldn't, if I were you,' Shelley grinned down at him, unabashed.

'With Janet off to Cairns tomorrow, I guess I'll hardly see you at all,' he bemoaned. 'Lynn won't be here to give you any help—Louise insists she go to Cairns in her place.'

'Luke, I'm young, fit and able,' she chided laughingly, and almost choked as an arm encircled her waist. It was Mitch—acting the devoted fiancé with complete conviction.

'Are you indeed?'

She turned and met the hidden laughter in the depths of his eyes, and pulled a face at him, tempering it with a smile for Luke's benefit. 'Of course,' she replied sweetly.

'Hmm,' he mused lazily. 'I think I'm being got at.'

'You are,' his father grinned irrepressibly.

'Circumstances don't permit suitable retaliation,' Mitch slanted quizzically, and Luke began to laugh.

Shelley tried to move away from that encircling arm only to have it tighten. 'I think Janet needs my help,' she said desperately.

'Come the day when you won't escape so easily, little one,' he murmured as he bent to touch his lips to her cheek.

'Play for me soon, Shelley?' Luke asked gently, and his eyes softened as he witnessed her confusion.

'We both will,' Mitch declared evenly as he allowed her to slip away.

Half an hour with Janet at the kitchen table sorted out what needed to be done towards Wednesday's preparations, and between them they wrote down a menu that would allow all the cooking to be done in the morning.

'The photographer is coming at three, the minister at four,' Janet recounted pensively. 'If we have hors d'oeuvres and champagne at five, followed by dinner at seven, then you and Mitch should be able to get away straight after Luke is settled into bed at nine,' she finished with satisfaction.

'Get away?' Shelley echoed aghast, and Janet smiled.

138

'You surely weren't planning on spending your wedding night here? Every spare room is occupied, and besides, while you're in Cairns it will give me the opportunity to get your bedroom furniture moved out and a double suite moved in. Afterwards when the others have gone you'll be able to choose which of the rooms you prefer.'

Shelley couldn't think of a thing to say right then —she doubted if her voice would have come out as anything other than a startled squeak.

'I'm going to visit my sister down south, after Luke——' Janet paused, unable to continue. 'Just for a month. It will give you and Mitch some time alone,' she concluded briskly.

Shelley felt her throat constrict painfully. All this talk of bedrooms and double beds sent her into a blind panic. Her knowledge of physical sex was entirely theoretical, and the mere thought of sharing such intimacies with Mitch was enough to set her emotions spiralling out of control. She almost wished that she *had* followed her sister-students' example and indulged in such games during her college years—at least now she wouldn't be an idiotic mass of nerves! That Mitch was a practised lover she didn't doubt for one moment, for he exuded virile masculinity from every nerve and fibre, and those dark eyes of tawny topaz held a latent sensuality that sent shivers up and down her spine.

With a certain measure of desperation she rose to her feet. 'I'd better go and play the guitar for Luke,' she managed with apparent calm. 'Are you coming?'

'I'll join you in a few minutes,' Janet essayed with a slight frown. 'I want to check this list out again— we may need more than I've ordered.'

Shelley slipped quickly through the doorway and moved down the hall, pausing to collect her instrument before entering the lounge.

Mitch chose to settle his lengthy frame on the arm of her chair just as soon as she began to play, and perforce she had to remain where she was. Consequently, she stumbled over several chords during the next half-hour that quite probably went undetected by their listening audience, but she knew Mitch was aware of each and every one of them!

It irked her no end that he deliberately sought to throw her into a state of confusion—she could tell by the teasing glint in his eyes, and in a fit of silent rage she waited until he returned from assisting Luke to bed.

Not even giving him time to sit down, she held out his guitar and begged him to play in a soft entreating voice. 'Please, darling. For me,' she added with seeming wistfulness. There, let him wriggle out of that one!

His eyes flared alive, dangerously so, for one brief second, then he took the instrument and after seating himself comfortably nearby began to play.

It was a spellbound ten minutes that seemed suspended in time, and when he put the guitar to one side it took her several seconds to alienate her self with her surroundings.

'Thank you,' she murmured, answering his sloping smile with one that was warm and altogether witching.

'My pleasure, little one.'

'Well, I'm for bed,' Louise declared, and stood gingerly to her feet, then with the aid of a stout walking stick she made her way slowly across the room. 'Lynn?'

'Yes—coming,' her daughter replied, and Hal got to his feet with a bored yawn, declaring his intention to retire with a book.

It almost seemed a conspiracy, Shelley thought idly, as Janet disappeared with the excuse of needing an early night.

'I'm going, too,' she voiced warily, not at all sure of the way Mitch was regarding her. Like a tiger browsing in the sun, ever watchful over its quarry.

She had to pass his chair on her way from the lounge, and as she drew level and was about to breathe a sigh of relief he reached out and caught hold of her hand, successfully halting her flight. With effortless ease he pulled her towards him until she touched the arm of his chair, and his eyes held a lazy gleam that foretold an intention to tease.

'Don't—please,' she protested, trying valiantly to extricate her hand.

'Why should you be so afraid of a harmless kiss or two?' he queried mildly.

Harmless? He had only to look at her and she melted into a thousand pieces, she thought wildly. If he kissed her, she'd be lost, a victim of her own emotions.

'Stop teasing, Mitch,' she pleaded desperately, then gasped out loud as he lifted her bodily on to his lap.

'Be still, child.'

'I'm not a child!' she hit out, feeling ridiculously hurt.

'Then behave like the grown-up woman you claim to be,' he commanded gently, one hand idly threading fingers through her hair to cup her nape while the other tilted her chin.

For several seconds he just looked down into that

endearing face, letting his eyes rove slowly over its delicately-moulded contours. Then he bent his head, his mouth seeking the delicate hollows at the base of her throat before trailing upwards to touch her cheekbone, each eyelid in turn before settling with gentle possession on her lips.

Being in his arms like this was sweet ecstasy, and after a few seconds Shelley was unaware of time. Of their own volition her arms crept up around his neck, and as the fingers of one hand encountered the ring on one finger of the other she felt a shaft of exultation expand within until her whole body and soul became enmeshed in sensual awareness. There was no doubting his expertise, nor her vulnerability beneath his touch.

It was he who slowly disengaged her arms and lifted his head to slant an incredibly tender smile as she buried her face against his throat.

'Bed, my innocent angel,' he bade softly, standing to his feet with easy fluidity. 'You, to dream pleasant dreams, while I seek solitary solace in the study with a stiff brandy.' So saying, he set her down gently and when she didn't move, turned her about and placed a brisk slap to her derriere. 'One foot in front of the other, hmm?'

Shelley almost floated as she walked towards the door, and glancing back blew him a witching kiss. 'Sleep well.'

'I very much doubt it,' he drawled mockingly, and those tantalising words stayed in her mind to become woven into her dreams.

# CHAPTER SEVEN

TUESDAY became a number of work-filled hours that passed with the seeming speed of minutes, and Shelley needed scant encouragement to slip off to her bed at the relatively early evening hour of nine-thirty. In spite of the conviction that she wouldn't sleep a wink, she fell asleep almost as soon as her head touched the pillow, and awoke when Janet called her at seven next morning.

'Breakfast in bed?' she couldn't help querying in slightly scandalised tones as Janet set a laden tray on the pedestal beside her bed.

'Tradition,' Janet declared laughingly, and Shelley proffered a rueful smile.

'Uh-huh. With more to come?'

'It gets worse as the day wears on,' came the twinkling reply, and Shelley reached out for her coffee, her eyes pensive.

'No matter what anyone says,' she began with determination, 'I'm not going to lie in bed until mid-morning, and then spend the remainder of the day leisurely tending to beauty ministrations. I need to keep occupied,' she ended on a desperate note, and there was conscious appeal in her voice. The day *had* to pass in a flurry of activity, otherwise she'd never get through it!

'Mitch has organised for a friend and his wife to come and lay out the food and champagne, *and* remain afterwards to take care of the dishes—so thoughtful,' Janet imparted. 'It means I can enjoy myself without any worries.'

'Yes,' Shelley murmured abstractedly as she nibbled at a piece of toast. She wasn't in the least hungry, and already the butterflies were beginning to beat a faint tattoo inside her stomach.

'We'll have an early lunch—eleven-thirty, I think,' Janet mused pensively. 'There's not a great deal to do this morning, thanks to your efforts yesterday. The rush will come in the early afternoon when everyone crowds each available bathroom. The time will fly.'

And fly it did, with Louise stage-managing everything and everyone in her best committee chairwoman fashion, undaunted by such a minor hindrance as a sprained ankle.

Shelley reflected hazily that it was no wonder a bride had little clear recollection of her wedding day—one's family and sheer nervous reaction took care of that! 'Never mind the day—what of the night?' a devilish imp whispered inside her brain, and such thoughts set the butterfly wings fluttering wildly so that she had to cleanse her face of make-up and begin from scratch again, her hands were so shaky!

She had seen Mitch only briefly at lunch, and he displayed no such qualms, appearing indomitable, his manner bland. And afterwards, when Lynn seemed to fuss unnecessarily, it had been Janet who proved a tower of strength, so that when the photographer arrived she was dressed and ready, outwardly calm.

'You look beautiful, child,' Janet complimented sincerely, and leant forward to bestow a kiss on the pale cool cheek, then stood back and there was a suspicious shimmer in those kindly eyes. 'You and Mitch are meant for each other—don't harbour the

144

slightest doubt, Shelley,' she commanded gently.

The girl reflected in the mirror seemed a stranger —the misty-eyed bride in the long white gown of silk voile, its bodice embroidered with white silk in the Greek style, and sleeves that were draped down to considerable width at each wrist. The neckline was cut in a deep square, and the skirt flowed in numerous flares to her feet.

'The photographer wants some shots in the gardens first, followed by some in the lounge,' Janet intimated, and Shelley moved with seeming automation, smiling when she was told to do so and posing as directed.

In no time at all she was walking slowly down a garland-bright aisle with Luke in his wheelchair at her side, moving steadily towards the small family group assembled in front of the jacaranda.

The minister contrived to instil some informality on an otherwise formal occasion, and conducted the ceremony in a friendly fashion with just the right amount of solemnity. He was young, new to his parish, and beamed delightedly when invited to stay for the wedding celebrations.

One glass of champagne on a relatively empty stomach had Shelley smiling rather fixedly. The wide gold band beneath her engagement ring proclaimed she was now Mrs Mitchell Ballantyne, a married woman who had solemnly repeated 'till death us do part' less than an hour before. It didn't seem real, nor did Mitch, looking so ruggedly handsome in a pale grey lounge-suit.

It all went so smoothly, so *quickly*, it seemed impossible that four hours had passed since she had walked through the gardens to stand at Mitch's side before the minister. She was aware of his warm hand clasping hers, and everything after that took on a dreamlike quality.

'Time to get changed, Shelley,' Mitch slanted quietly beside her, his smile warm. 'Then we'll have some coffee and get on our way.'

She looked up at him in mute consternation, the smile fading rapidly as her eyes widened incredulously.

'Can you manage, or do you need some help?' he queried, then added with sharply drawn breath, 'not mine—Lynn's, or preferably Janet's.' His eyes seemed to narrow and become hard.

'Yes—no,' she stumbled incoherently, then clarified with a muttered—'I can manage.' With that she slipped from the lounge, aware that he was following close behind.

A change of clothes was already laid out on her bed, Janet's helping hand without doubt, and her overnight bag had disappeared from beside the wardrobe. With shaky fingers Shelley removed her veil, slipped out of her shoes, and reached a hand over her shoulder to tackle the zip fastener. It slid smoothly down past her shoulder-blades, then slowed to a halt. Darn—it jolly well would! she cursed beneath her breath. She coaxed it gently up and then down, but it stubbornly refused to budge.

Trying not to panic, she endeavoured to ease the gown down without success. No matter what she did nothing freed the fastener, and she felt herself become flushed with fruitless exertion. It was almost a relief when she heard the bedroom door open.

'Oh, thank heavens!' she exclaimed anxiously. 'Janet, be a dear—this darn zip has stuck.'

'Stand still, child,' a slow drawl bade wryly from close behind, and the next minute she felt the fleet-

146

ing touch of Mitch's warm fingers on her bare skin. The 'child' rankled, and she turned her head slightly.

'I thought it was Janet,' she flung vexedly, only to have a hand at her shoulder force her to stand straight.

'Only your husband stopping by to see if you were ready,' Mitch intoned dryly. 'It would be best if we both went back into the lounge together, don't you think?'

Shelley didn't answer—she couldn't. She was too conscious of his close proximity and the warmth of his fingers as they brushed, albeit impersonally, against her spine. Just as she thought she'd begin trembling from sheer nerves, there was a sudden feeling of release as the fastener became free.

'I'll turn my back,' came cryptically from behind, and she bit back a sharp retort.

With admirable speed she slipped out of the gown, pulled a wispy slip over her head before shedding the long half-slip she had worn beneath her gown, and hastily donned the skirt, top and jacket that was on her bed. A few minutes spent tidying up, then several brisk strokes of the brush to her hair, a touch of lipstick, and she was ready.

In the lounge she was overly bright, trying hard to appear vivacious and happy, and the tears in Luke's eyes as she bent to kiss him brought a shimmering brightness to her own.

'I'm more happy than I can say,' Luke proclaimed softly. 'Take care,' he directed Mitch, then smiled gently. 'God bless you both.'

As Mitch slid the car into gear they were fondly farewelled by the small group from the verandah, and Shelley waved until they were almost out of sight.

'Relax, little one,' Mitch drawled. 'I'm not about to eat you.'

The car turned on to the main road, quickly gathering speed.

'I didn't imagine you would,' Shelley replied coolly, and she sensed his wry smile.

'I can read you like a book, or had you forgotten?' he queried with dry amusement, and when she deigned not to answer, he shot her a quick discerning glance. 'There are times when I find myself hard pressed not to place you across my knee!'

'You wouldn't dare!' she flung incautiously, knowing full well that he would, given sufficient provocation.

'Continue pursuing your present train of thought,' he warned silkily, and she tossed him an angry glance.

'You could be wrong.'

'I doubt it.'

At such wry cynicism she fell silent, and gazed unseeing out at the dark looming shapes outside the car window. The moon silvered the ocean's velvet-smooth surface, casting ghostlike shadows obliquely across the sand, and magnifying the density of the surrounding bush.

Dear God, she pleaded silently. Why can't I admit how much he means to me—that without him, I'm nothing? Why do Louise's words keep hammering a persistent echo inside my brain? 'So right, this marriage—it takes care of what could have proved an awkward situation.' Now, with every passing minute she was forcing the gap wider between them.

As the large car covered the miles she became

increasingly nervous, sure that something drastic had happened to her vocal cords. Twice she tried to urge her voice to ask Mitch to turn round the car and take her back, but not a sound came out. If only she could go home, she despaired—home to her own room, her own bed. All her instincts had gone awry, so sure had she been that this marriage would never eventuate. She had allowed herself to be lulled into a state of false security in the desire to please Luke, and the shallows had slowly disappeared along with the safe shore. No doubt about the deep water and the huge swelling sea she had floated into now. *Floated* was the operative word!

The lights of Cairns glimmered in the distance, and there seemed to be a steady stream of opposing traffic until the car skirted the main city route and swung off on to the Esplanade.

'I hardly dare ask, your expression eludes me in this light.' Mitch's low faintly amused voice penetrated her thoughts, capturing her attention with a jolt.

'Are we there?' A silly question if ever there was one, for the car was stationary.

'Stay there while I collect the key,' he instructed, slipping out from the car with ease, and Shelley watched his tall frame move towards the lighted front office.

They each had an overnight bag in the boot, and for the sake of something to do, she slid out from her seat and moved to the rear of the car. His was the lighter of the two, and she doubted it held much more than toiletries. Oh, dear Lord, why had she allowed herself to be managed and manoeuvred into this—situation?

She became aware of him locking the car, taking

both bags from her nerveless hands, and the deep probing look he cast in her direction as he firmly gripped her elbow.

Their unit was modern, luxuriously furnished, and large, Shelley noticed as she followed him into the lounge, and she hovered hesitantly just inside the doorway of the bedroom as he deposited their bags on the floor.

'I suppose if I ask which bed you'd prefer,' he drawled, 'you'll take several steps backwards and flee the room.'

She eyed him warily, then managed a light shrug. 'I don't suppose it matters much, anyway,' she voiced quietly.

His silence became intense, electrifying the air between them. 'We've known each other ten years, Shelley,' he stated dangerously, 'yet all of a sudden I seem to frighten the very wits from you. Why?'

The vexed look she flung him was pure self-defence. 'There you go again, implying that I'm little more than a child,' she sallied resentfully.

'Aren't you?' His query was a sardonic drawl and she blushed beneath his mocking gaze.

When she didn't answer, his eyes darkened into topaz flints. 'Have whichever bed you like, Shelley. The room is yours.' With that he retrieved his bag and left the room.

A chill swept round the region of her heart, encasing it in ice. Dully, she heard the television from the lounge, and concluded that he'd found the electronic entertainment an improvement on their verbal dissension.

Summoning every ounce of courage she possessed, she began unpacking the contents of her overnight bag, then took the brush to her hair and stroked its length with hard vigorous strokes until her scalp tingled and her arm ached. Then, before she could give it second thought, she moved towards the lounge and sat down in an armchair a few feet distant from the one Mitch occupied.

Images flashed across the screen, but she saw little. After an interminable length of time she glanced over at him with an anxious, troubled expression, for she hated being at odds with him for long, and almost as if he sensed her inner turmoil he swung his gaze towards her.

'If you have something to say,' he said wryly, 'get it over with, little one. I don't intend meditating the complexities of the female mind for much longer.'

She cleared her throat, then voiced wretchedly, 'You don't have to sleep out here.'

The look he spared her was wholly cynical. 'No?' He stood slowly to his feet and ran a hand wearily through his hair. 'Something alcoholic might ease things a little,' and with this dry statement he left the room to return with a bottle of champagne in his hand.

'Shall we?' His query was mild enough, although his eyes narrowed fractionally as he glimpsed her nervousness.

'Why not?' Shelley countered with forced lightness, and escaped into the kitchen to fetch two glasses.

Mitch opened the bottle with calculated ease and filled each glass to the brim. 'To us,' he declared seriously, raising his glass to touch hers before putting it to his lips, when all Shelley could do was smile rather tremulously.

'You're as nervous as a kitten,' he observed, albeit

gently. 'Will it help if I assure you have no reason to be?'

She longed to cry out baldly—'Why did you marry me? Was it because it seemed the convenient thing to do? Is it too much to want to be loved and needed for myself—not married off as a solution to an awkward situation?' But she couldn't voice those words, and somehow she managed a shaky smile.

'You'll have to make allowances, Mitch.'

'Believe me—with you, I make them all the time,' he slanted lazily, and reaching out he ran an idle finger down her cheek, declaring softly, 'Your eyes are like saucers.'

She swallowed nervously, and endeavoured to concentrate on appearing calm. She had as much chance of assuming that state as she had of jumping over the moon! 'It's not every day a girl gets married,' she offered at last.

'And there's any number of mixed-up thoughts racing through that mind of yours, hmm?' he queried tolerantly. 'Come and watch television for a while—I doubt either one of us is in the mood for sleep.' With a slight smile he led her towards the settee, pausing until she was seated before bending his lengthy frame down beside her.

Shelley sipped the contents of her glass, all too aware of the casually-placed arm about her shoulders as she attempted to concentrate on an episode depicting American police detection.

After a while her eyelids began to droop so that she had to make a conscious effort to keep them open. The events of the past few days were making themselves felt, and soon she gave in to the irresistible desire to doze.

She was unaware of Mitch's slow smile, or of the

arms that lifted and carried her to the bedroom, and she remained blissfully asleep as he placed her down on to one of the two single beds, removed her shoes, then gently slid off her skirt and jacket before covering her with the counterpane.

The need for a glass of water to quench her thirst roused Shelley into wakefulness, and she lay there momentarily unsure of her surroundings. Then it all flooded back, and it was several minutes before she could bring herself to glance cautiously around the dimness of the room. That Mitch had for some unknown reason changed his mind and elected to occupy the other bed was obvious, and at the sound of his steady breathing she uttered a silent sigh of relief.

Slowly she eased herself out of bed and padded stealthily out to the kitchen. She could just make out the outline of a glass on the bench, and picking it up carefully she cautiously filled it from the tap. Ah, that was good—champagne always did make her thirsty. Now, to get back and slip into bed.

She crept back into the bedroom and was about to slide beneath the covers when it struck her that she was still partially clothed. Retrieving the night-gown she had placed beneath the pillows several hours earlier, she carefully shed her slip, then bra and panties before donning the frivolous concoction of nylon and lace. Sparing a quick glance in the direction of the other bed she saw that Mitch was still fast asleep, and with a slight smile she turned back to slide between the sheets.

'Oh!' Her startled gasp sounded loud in the night's silence as a hand reached out and grasped her arm. Her surprise was such that she didn't think to struggle as she was pulled gently down on to the opposite bed, and it was only when she felt the warmth of his body next to hers that she became aware of the consequences of his actions.

Mitch's softly-voiced—'yes'—as she attempted to escape set her limbs trembling, and her heart began an elevated erratic tattoo. This was madness! A madness she couldn't afford.

His touch was gentle, his lips trailing lingeringly across the edge of her shoulder, caressing the delicate hollows beneath her throat before finding her mouth with unerring accuracy.

Oh, dear God, she moaned silently. Nothing seemed to matter any more. Of their own volition her lips parted and she melted beneath his sensual expertise.

There was a distant ringing in her ears, she decided languorously, and her arms tightened fractionally as she felt Mitch make an attempt to move away.

'The telephone,' he murmured huskily, sliding from the bed in one fluid movement, grabbing a robe off the end of the bed before moving quickly from the room.

Shelley lay supine, savouring a wonderful floating sensation. Right at this moment she didn't care what had motivated their marriage. She loved him so much there was no denying him anything.

Suddenly she jack-knifed from the bed as the implication of what that unheralded middle-of-the-night telephone call must mean. Luke! Hurriedly she flung arms into the lacy peignoir she'd packed, then fled swiftly to the lounge to stand at Mitch's side. At once his arm drew her close, and she stood there with an awful sense of foreboding as she detected the seriousness in his voice.

'It's Luke, isn't it?' she asked quietly when he replaced the receiver, and it wasn't really a question at all.

'That was Janet—he's suffering another attack,' Mitch answered bleakly.

'I'll pack,' Shelley said immediately, and moved quickly back to the bedroom where she donned slacks and a short-sleeved top, then hastily flung everything else into her bag. Mitch was doing the same, and there wasn't time for conversation. Even when they had left the motel behind and were travelling at considerable speed along the coast road there seemed nothing to say, for their thoughts were entirely taken up with anxiety over Luke.

Light blazed out from the homestead and spilled on to the lawn as the car pulled in beside the verandah. The doctor's car was parked close by, and as they mounted the steps Janet appeared.

Shelley couldn't bring herself to ask how bad Luke was, or if they had arrived too late, and she acquiesced silently as Mitch bade her go with Janet into the kitchen.

Louise was seated at the table pouring tea into a cup, and she looked tired and strained, as did Janet.

'Have some tea, Shelley,' Janet instructed gently. 'It looks like being a long night.'

'How long has the doctor been here?' Shelley asked as she spooned sugar into her cup and added milk.

'Twenty minutes or so. I expect he'll leave soon. There won't be much he can do,' Louise stated sadly.

Shelley drank her tea quickly, then poured another cup. 'I'll take this through to Mitch.'

The doctor was about to leave as she reached

Luke's bedroom door, and she quietly bade him go into the kitchen where Janet would give him coffee or tea, whichever he preferred.

Mitch was standing beside the bed when she entered, and as she handed him the tea in silence she glimpsed Emma on the other side of the room. At first she thought Luke was asleep, then realised he had lapsed into unconsciousness.

'I'll stay,' Shelley whispered some time later when Mitch indicated that she should go to bed, and Emma, having recently returned from the kitchen, endorsed his decision.

'There's little you can do,' the nurse declared firmly, adding, 'Mr Ballantyne is deeply unconscious and quite unaware of anyone here.'

'If he—wakes——' Shelley voiced hesitantly, and received Emma's pitying stare.

'I'll come and fetch you,' Mitch reassured steadily.

Needless to say he didn't, and Shelley awoke next morning to find the light streaming through her window. A glance at her watch showed it was well after nine, and she positively leapt from her bed to dress hurriedly before seeking Mitch, Janet— someone, for news of Luke.

The kitchen seemed the obvious room in which to begin, and she found Janet clearing dishes from the table. One look at her sad, weary face told Shelley all she needed to know.

'A few hours ago,' the older woman disclosed gently. 'Mitch thought it best to let you sleep.'

Shelley's eyes filled with tears and her throat began to ache with pent-up emotion.

'It was just a matter of time, Shelley. We all know that,' Janet said quietly, adding, 'Mitch has gone into town.'

Shelley nodded disconsolately. 'I think I'll go out into the gardens for a while.' She needed to be alone with her thoughts, for if she stayed inside another minute she'd burst into tears.

It was there that Mitch found her, more than an hour later, pulling weeds from the soil with serious dedication.

'Janet tells me you haven't had breakfast,' he began without preamble, and she shook her head, unable to look at him. Her eyes felt achey and not quite her own from recent tears.

'I'm not hungry,' she maintained abstractedly as she plucked a withered leaf from a nearby shrub.

'You'll eat something, nonetheless.'

'Don't bully me, Mitch. I couldn't bear it,' she said shakily.

'Then be a good girl and come inside. Share my coffee,' he ordered gently, and without a word she fell into step beside him.

'I don't suppose you've had much sleep?' she ventured tentatively.

'None.'

'You must,' she declared positively, and caught his slight smile.

'Now who's bullying who?'

'So must Janet,' she continued, ignoring his wry query. 'I doubt she's been to bed at all.'

In the kitchen there was a meal ready for them both, and in spite of Shelley's plea that she wasn't hungry, she ate well, pouring a second cup of coffee from the pot as she persuaded Janet to get a few hours sleep.

Soon after Janet had gone, Mitch stood to his feet, and Shelley shot him a look of concern.

'I'm going to wash the dishes, then begin preparing lunch. I'll keep yours warm in the oven and you can have it when you wake.'

'My, my,' Hal drawled slowly from the doorway. 'Such wifely devotion!'

'Two hours, Shelley,' Mitch declared evenly. 'Wake me if I'm not up by then.'

'Bit of bad luck,' Hal observed cynically as he sat down at the table after Mitch had left the room.

Shelley began stacking dishes and made a monosyllabic reply.

'Never mind. You'll have the house to yourselves soon,' Hal uttered sardonically, and poured himself some coffee. 'We're all taking off straight after the funeral, and the good Emma is driving down to Cairns with us to save Mitch an extra trip.'

'Is Lynn up yet?' she asked, determined to change the subject.

'No—she and Mother look set to sleep the morning away. Likewise Janet and Emma, not forgetting your dear husband,' he finished dryly, only to add seconds later, 'Funny—you don't look like a dewy-eyed bride. Dare I conclude my redoubtable cousin didn't make first base last night?'

'I suspect you'd dare anything,' Shelley said with heavy sarcasm.

'Rather convenient, this marriage,' he continued as if she hadn't spoken. 'You must have hidden charms, sweetheart, to have hooked the mighty Mitchell Ballantyne. He always did have an eye for the girls—they fall like ninepins,' he laughed callously. 'And he has everything—looks, money, charm. Yet he chose you—or did he? Perhaps you're more clever than I thought.'

Shelley felt the anger burn within her, and she

158

endeavoured to retain a semblance of calm. 'Jealousy will get you nowhere.'

'Jealous of the Ballantyne fortunes, my dear girl, nothing more. I also have looks, and enough savoir faire to charm any number of birds from the trees—not the feathered kind, you understand?'

'You disgust me,' she declared bluntly as she set about washing the sink full of dishes with unnecessary dedication. Honestly, if Hal didn't remove his presence soon, she'd throw something at him!

'Some of the human race are disgusting, one way or another—or haven't you discovered that yet?' he drawled cynically.

'Be judged as you judge others,' she uttered succinctly, and victory was very sweet.

'You're too goody-goody, Shelley Anderson-Ballantyne—like the tooth-fairy. You'll get your come-uppance one day, and I hope I'm around to see it!'

'I'll send you an invitation,' Shelley offered, trying hard not to become rattled.

'Perhaps Mitch will decide he wants more spice than you're capable of giving, and divorce you for someone more accommodating.'

That hit a raw nerve, and she retaliated without thinking, rounding on him with sheer fury. 'How can you be so horrid? Haven't you an ounce of respect?' she expostulated witheringly. 'When you've finished your coffee, please remove yourself from the kitchen,' she finished repressively, sure that if he stayed she'd end up hitting him.

'With pleasure! When you wake my cousin, you can tell him I've helped myself to a vehicle and gone into town.' His chair scraped back on the floor, then he strode over to the bench and slammed his cup and saucer into the sink, sending a spray of hot sudsy water all over the top half of her dress and up into her face.

Shelley felt her eyes smart, and with shaking hands she wet the edge of a cloth with clean water and attempted to bathe them. There were tears mingling in there as well, and she was more shaken up than she cared to admit. How anyone, especially someone related to Luke, could be so deliberately malicious at such a time was beyond her comprehension. She was in her room changing her clothes when she heard the utility truck take off at a fast rate down the drive, and she uttered a silent plea that he wouldn't return until dinner was ready that evening. Perhaps she'd get lucky and he'd stay in town until the hotels closed at ten o'clock.

The desire to collapse on to her bed and indulge in a bout of weeping was very tempting. Everyone said it was best to have a good cry rather than bottle things up. But if she started she had the feeling she wouldn't stop for quite a while, and there were still the dishes to finish, a meal to prepare. Work was supposed to be a good panacea for emotional upsets, she mused. Well, there was plenty she could do!

The day passed surprisingly quickly, and fortunately there was no sign of Hal. He didn't put in an appearance for dinner that evening, either, and Shelley began to feel hopeful that she might be well in bed by the time he returned. Luke's funeral had been arranged for early the following afternoon, and Louise declared her intention to return south immediately after the service.

There was a particularly poignant moment after dinner when everyone gathered in the lounge, for it was then Luke's absence was most noticed. It made Shelley feel incredibly sad and all too aware of how much she loved the kindly man who had been like a father these past ten years. Thinking of the good times they had shared, his generosity, his love, brought a lump to her throat and an ache within.

She had hardly seen Mitch all day except at meal-times, and straight after dinner he disappeared into the study, only to emerge shortly after nine with a rather grim expression on his face when he dis-covered Hal hadn't returned.

'I'd better go into town and fetch him back,' he indicated curtly to Louise. 'I'll take Ken with me. It's highly probable he won't be in a fit state to drive,' he added with asperity.

'I daresay the dear boy is upset,' Louise attempted to pour oil on troubled waters and received a hard stare from Mitch.

'Aren't we all?' he drawled bluntly, his dark eyes glittering dangerously.

He's fighting mad, Shelley deduced thoughtfully, not envying Hal in the slightest when Mitch got hold of him!

'Well, of course,' Louise answered quickly. 'Per-haps I should come with you.'

Mitch's expression was sufficient to restore her half-risen figure back into the chair, and with a curt monosyllabic refusal he left the lounge. Minutes later they heard the sedan purr into life and speed down the driveway.

'I think Mitch is over-reacting,' Louise offered with the air of a mother whose son can do no wrong, and Lynn shot her a rueful smile.

'Mother—really! Mitch is quite within his rights to be angry. Hal should be here, not drinking him-self into oblivion in a pub. And besides, he shouldn't have driven off like that,' she concluded.

'It's been difficult for him,' Louise explained patiently. 'He's not at all in tune with country life.'

Amen to that, Shelley echoed silently, casting a quick glance at her watch. 'If nobody minds, I think I'll have an early night. I've been nursing a headache all day, and the sooner I get my head down the better,' she asserted tiredly. It had been a long night, followed by a difficult day, and she longed for a bit of solitude. Besides, it might be best if she was already in bed and asleep by the time Mitch returned with Hal in tow.

'Poor thing,' Lynn sympathised. 'You've had a difficult time of it.'

'A small brandy wouldn't do us any harm,' Louise declared briskly. 'We've all been under an incredible strain this past week.'

'I'll get some glasses,' Janet declared wearily. 'Somehow I think an early night for us all would be a good idea.'

'No brandy for me,' Shelley said, giving a prodigious yawn. 'Oh, excuse me. I really must go to bed,' she essayed, standing to her feet. 'Goodnight.'

It was heavenly to slip between the sheets of her comfortable bed, and she was far too tired to ponder over anything. Within minutes she was fast asleep, and dreamt on through Hal's noisy return, oblivious to all.

She was unaware of Mitch coming into her room and standing beside the bed for an interminable length of time, and it was doubtful she felt the gentle kiss he bestowed to each eyelid and at the corner of her mouth before crossing the hall to his solitary divan in the study.

# CHAPTER EIGHT

SHELLEY awoke at first light feeling refreshed from a sound night's sleep, and after hastily donning slacks and a knit top she made for the bathroom. It looked like being another warm day, for the sky was clear and light.

She wandered into the kitchen and boiled the kettle to make a cup of instant coffee, moving as quietly as she could. There wasn't a sound in the house, and it was doubtful if anyone else was awake, let alone up. She wondered idly how Hal had fared —he would be nursing a massive hangover this morning that wouldn't have been helped by Mitch's icy anger, or Louise's disfavour.

It was too early to do anything yet, except set the breakfast table, and when that was done she opened the side door to let Bessie in for her early morning snack.

'Spoilt rotten, my girl,' Shelley whispered affectionately, and the dog wagged its tail in complete agreement as it lapped warm milk. 'Come on, Bess, we'll go for a walk and savour the silence before the air is rent with the sound of machinery,' she added softly, and Bessie needed no second bidding.

Together they made their way from the verandah down through the gardens to the edge of the paddock, following the grassed tracks. It was so fresh and clean at this early hour, the sun's rays directing a soft warmth on the earth below, giving it a newness in the still morning air. This was Luke's land, the soil he'd tilled and planted year after year, building up a vast acreage with the sweat of hard labour. There was a whole life's work expended on this land, and there would be many more to follow. Mitch's son, and in turn his son. To think of this being anything other than Ballantyne land was inconceivable. Perhaps that was the reason for life on earth—to enjoy to the fullest and gain satisfaction out of achieving something totally worthwhile, with everything along the way being a test of strength both mental and physical. Oh, Luke, she breathed softly, hugging her arms together across her body, thank you for sharing—allowing me to be a part of all this.

Bessie gave a low canine woof, and Shelley looked across towards Ken's cottage where the back door was standing open. He was there in the doorway, and she waved, smiling as he waved back and beckoned her across.

'You're out early,' Ken smiled that wide slow smile of his. 'Made your peace, have you?' he queried gently.

'Yes,' she said simply, smiling with inner contentment as she followed him into the kitchen and began to chuckle softly as Bessie trotted over to share Mutt's warm milk. Ken took down another mug and poured fresh coffee, adding milk and sugar before passing it to her. 'The house will seem empty after today,' he ventured thoughtfully.

'It will seem even emptier while Janet is away,' she said quietly, then changed the subject. 'I believe you had to perform a rescue of sorts last night?'

'Hal? We found him the worse for wear, and in need of persuasion to come home,' he grinned in retrospect, savouring the memory with a certain satisfaction.

'Mitch was unsympathetic, I gather?'

He saw the twinkle in her eyes and matched it with one of his own. 'You could say that.'

Shelley sipped her coffee and cast an affectionate glance down at Bessie as she padded over to her chair and flopped down with her head on her paws.

'The nurse is going back today?' Ken's casual query captured her attention, and something in his tone caused her to look searchingly into those kindly blue eyes.

'I think so. Janet mentioned something of the sort yesterday. It will save Mitch an extra trip, to take her when he drives the others down,' she added pensively.

'Good.'

Her eyes widened slightly and the beginnings of a frown creased her forehead. 'You don't like her?'

'I don't trust women in general.'

'No exceptions?' Her lips parted in an impish smile.

'Oh, one or two,' he allowed with a chuckle.

'But not Emma Stone,' Shelley concluded, and Ken shook his head slowly. 'Well, I can't say she's exactly my cup of tea either. Anyway, she won't be around after today.'

'I daresay there'll be a crowd back at the house this afternoon,' he commented thoughtfully. 'Luke was well liked, and a respected man.'

At the mention of Luke's name, Bessie gave a whimper and turned her head to regard Shelley with an incredibly sad look in her large spaniel's eyes.

'She knows,' Ken declared softly, and she nodded in agreement.

'Animal instinct,' she alleged.

At that moment there was the sound of a tractor starting in the sheds several hundred yards away, and the noise grew louder as it roared down the track.

'Mitch,' Ken deduced with a slow smile at Shelley's surprised expression. 'Stay and finish your coffee,' he instructed as she hurriedly picked up her mug.

'No, I must get back. Thanks, Ken.'

She reached the door just as Mitch leapt down from the tractor, and at once her stomach curled alarmingly. 'Good morning,' she managed steadily, then almost choked as he planted a brief hard kiss on her unsuspecting lips.

''morning,' he answered imperturbably, and his tawny eyes held hidden laughter as they witnessed her startled expression. 'Ken's not blushing, little one—why should you?' he teased, and she shot him a glance that had no effect whatever.

He really was impossible, and it was on the tip of her tongue to tell him so. However, the opportunity was lost, for he climbed back behind the wheel of the tractor, and Ken jumped quickly on to the cultivating machine connected to its rear. Then they were gone and she was left to gaze after them.

Well, it was no good to stand here idly, she breathed deeply. Breakfast was less than an hour away, and after that Janet would need help in preparing sandwiches, scones and such like for the considerable number of people who would return to the house after the funeral service this afternoon.

Neither Louise nor Hal showed up for breakfast, and Lynn cast Mitch a rueful smile as she sat down at the table.

'Mother begs to be excused—a headache, you

know. My dear brother is in no fit shape to declare a need for food or otherwise,' she grimaced as she poured herself some coffee.

'I thought you handled everything splendidly last night,' Emma directed across the table to Mitch, who made no comment as he cut into the thick steak on his plate. 'It could have turned into something quite nasty,' she continued. 'He was very belligerent.'

'An unpleasant episode best forgotten, I think,' Mitch asserted silkily, and Shelley couldn't help but see the girl's eyes narrow in anger at his deliberate snub.

'Are you going back to the paddock?' Janet asked with apparent unconcern, and Shelley hid a slight smile as she recognised the other's attempt to change the subject.

'Until eleven. Lunch a little early, perhaps?' Mitch glanced sideways and received her nod of agreement, then returned his attention to Emma. 'The car will be leaving for Cairns around five this afternoon.'

The nurse's lips thinned a little, although the smile she gave him was tinged with just the right amount of regret. 'I'm in no hurry to get back. Tomorrow or Sunday would do just as well.'

Shelley didn't dare glance at Mitch, or at Janet. She took a bite of toast and chewed it slowly, listening with fascination for his reply. It came after a few seconds' silence, an electric silence that almost set the air crackling in the room.

'It would mean having Ken make a special trip,' he dismissed politely, and doubtless Emma was the only one who failed to detect the icy undertone in his voice.

Shelley had to give Emma credit for trying, for the girl manufactured a gentle smile and said in an even gentler voice, 'I'm aware that my nursing assignment here has come to an end.'

'A job well done,' Mitch accorded pleasantly. 'Shall we say late this afternoon?'

'Thank you,' the nurse replied briefly, but it was plain she was disappointed, and Shelley could only wonder at what she hoped to achieve by staying.

After the breakfast dishes had been dealt with Shelley drove into Mossman to collect several loaves of fresh bread from the bakery with which to make sandwiches, and when she returned Janet was preparing a second batch of scones.

Lunch was a rather solemn meal, quickly eaten, as the church service was due to begin at one o'clock.

There were people spilling out from the lounge into the hall and on to the verandah, and a sizeable number were mingling on the lawn, Shelley observed, pleased that so many had chosen to show their respects. Nearly everyone for miles around had attended the service, but only a fraction came on to the house.

Even so, there must be at least fifty people here. She had lost sight of Mitch over half an hour ago; Janet and Lynn had stationed themselves in the kitchen and were hectically engaged in dispensing innumerable cups of tea and coffee. There were empty glasses everywhere, but it was a bit precipitate to begin collecting them.

The afternoon had been something of a strain in more ways than one, for news of Mitch's marriage to Shelley had travelled quickly. She had shaken so many hands and smiled at well-wishers until she felt

168

completely enervated, and with a politely-muttered excuse that her help was needed in the kitchen, she escaped.

Janet looked quite flustered, and there were empty plates in neat stacks covering most of the bench.

'Help is at hand,' Shelley announced brightly as she joined them, and was soon running hot water into the sink with which to tackle the gargantuan pile of crockery.

Half an hour later the kitchen was set to rights and ready to cope with the next onslaught, and Shelley bade Janet and Lynn mingle with the guests for a while.

'I'll join you soon—promise,' she added smilingly as Janet whipped off her apron and tidied her hair.

From the sound of car doors it appeared that a steady trickle of guests were departing, and a glance at her watch revealed that it was well after four o'clock. It wouldn't be long before Mitch left for Cairns, and when he returned ... Well, there would be time to ask those questions for which she needed answers. Perhaps after all there was a chance to build something out of this marriage, she thought pensively.

A light tap of feminine heels crossing the kitchen floor caused her to glance round, and her heart sank as she saw Emma advancing towards her carrying a tray of empty glasses.

'I thought I'd bring these,' Emma stated cursorily as she placed the tray on the bench. 'Everyone seems to be leaving.'

Shelley regarded her warily. There was a brittleness in the other girl's manner, a certain amount of pent-up ill-feeling that was disquieting.

Emma turned slightly, her appraisal insolent as she stood regarding Shelley. 'You certainly know which side your bread is buttered, don't you?'

'Precisely what do you mean?' Shelley countered watchfully.

'Mrs Mitchell Ballantyne,' Emma said slowly. 'My, my—what a clever piece of strategy it took to coax Mitch into marrying *you*!'

'I don't see that it's any of your business,' Shelley answered coldly as she endeavoured to control her irritation, and the nurse gave a short derisive laugh.

'You know, I could hardly believe my luck when this nursing assignment fell into my lap,' she revealed deliberately. 'The Ballantynes, with all their wealth and property,' she continued in disparaging tones, her eyes glittering maliciously. 'I had a chance, just a sporting chance I'll grant you, of inveigling the eminently eligible Mitchell, and I worked hard, incredibly hard, at being the self-effacing, virtuous nurse. Why,' she paused bitterly, 'I loathed you before you even appeared on the scene. All Luke Ballantyne could talk about was you—how wonderful you were, how beautiful. It made me sick in my stomach!'

'Have you finished?' Shelley queried icily, feeling surprisingly calm.

'Not quite!' Emma declared savagely. 'This quick marriage of yours was one big picture puzzle with some pieces out of place until I connected it to your bequest—inheritance is more like it! I was outside on the verandah the morning Luke Ballantyne revealed that piece of information,' she said caustically. 'I guess that was the carrot he dangled in front of his son's rather splendid nose. You are quite attractive in a cool sort of way—virginal, almost.

That look appeals to some men, and you are re-markably *domesticated*, as well as being able to strum a guitar for amusement's sake. Oh yes,' she evinced cynically, her head to one side, 'you'll make a satisfactory wife for appearances' sake, but hardly so in the bedroom, I'll be bound. Poor Mitch—an untried, prim little puritan for a wife!' she laughed cruelly, and turning round, she swept towards the door—only to have her way barred by Ken.

He just stood there with a thunderous expression on his face, and Shelley reflected numbly that in all the years she'd known him, not once had she seen anything remotely resembling anger on his placid features.

'Will you let me pass?' Emma hissed furiously, and she stood there defiantly as he raked her from head to toe before stepping aside.

Shelley cast him an incredibly stricken look. 'I suppose you heard some of it?'

'Enough,' he said brusquely.

'She's——'

'—a thorough bitch,' Ken concluded, his eyes holding hers unwaveringly.

'The things she said——' Shelley began ab-stractedly.

'Hogwash,' he denounced unequivocally. 'You know it.'

She looked up at him, feeling indescribably for-lorn. 'Do I?'

'Yes, Shelley,' he said with quiet emphasis, his eyes narrowing as she lifted shaking fingers to the slim gold chain at her throat. 'Mitch sent me to fetch you outside,' he told her gently. 'There are only a few close friends left, and they're ready to leave.'

171

'I can't——' she began desperately.

'You must,' he said with quiet authority, giving her a smile.

'I feel like a ghost,' she exclaimed wretchedly. 'They'll see——'

'No one expects sparkling conversation,' he said kindly. 'If anyone does take a second look, it will only be concluded to be grief over Luke.' He gave her a gentle push. 'Now, go.'

She managed it, although heaven knew how. Certainly it was the most difficult piece of acting she had ever attempted. Ten minutes seemed like ten hours, and when the last car had gone she walked back into the house like an automaton.

Feeling like something out of a dream she began gathering glasses, straightening chairs, collecting ashtrays, despite Janet's admonition to leave it all until after Mitch had left.

Shelley was hardly aware of the penetrating glance Mitch spared her body before moving down the steps to slip behind the wheel of the sedan.

Even Lynn's quietly-voiced, 'Roberto is flying down to Sydney soon. He has said he'll contact me,' brought scarcely a glimmer of a smile to her lips, and she murmured something appropriate, although what she had no recollection.

'We'll just have cold chicken and a salad for dinner, I think,' Janet declared as she stood beside Shelley on the verandah, waving until the car was out of sight. 'Mitch will be gone all of two hours. We should have things back to normal by then,' she paused with a smile. 'Even rearrange some furniture with Ken's help. A new bedroom suite arrived this morning while you were in town.'

That was the living end, and the tears began

trickling unchecked down Shelley's cheeks.

'Why, child——' Janet began gently.

'I can't stay here—not any more,' Shelley began wretchedly, shaking her head as Janet began to argue. 'No—you don't understand.'

'You're darned right I don't understand. What on earth has happened, child?'

'I have to get away,' Shelley said desperately.

'Mitch intends driving down to Cairns tomorrow for a few days,' Janet began placatingly. 'By the time you come back I'll have left—Ken is driving me down on Sunday. You're all upset over Luke, which is natural. But when Mitch comes back——'

'I meant me, alone.'

'You're leaving?' Janet queried, and there was a glimmer of anxiety evident in her expression.

'If—if you want to put it like that,' Shelley answered shakily, and Janet shook her head in perplexity.

'How do you think Mitch will react to that?'

'Be relieved, I guess,' Shelley offered obliquely.

'You're legally married,' Janet reminded her sternly as Shelley searched for and found a handkerchief.

'That was contrived for Luke's benefit,' she advised huskily, blowing her nose.

'Ten years you've known Mitch, and yet you can say that? Believe it?' Janet asked incredulously.

Shelley met her eyes steadily. 'I need time to think. I can't just wait here for him to come back,' she said slowly.

'Why not?'

'I couldn't live with myself, knowing Luke had persuaded Mitch to marry me out of some misguided sense of duty.' ‑

'Oh, Shelley, what utter nonsense! Who implied such a thing?' When Shelley didn't answer Janet queried gently, 'Can you imagine Mitch letting you go?'

'Why shouldn't he?' she asked sadly.

'Ah, child, I can't make you stay here,' Janet essayed worriedly. 'But I strongly advise you not to do anything rash until he gets back. It's been difficult for both of you—there's been very little time to talk, let alone anything else.'

'It's no good, Janet. I've made up my mind,' she said quietly. 'I'll help with the glasses, then I'll go.'

'Where?'

Shelley didn't answer, for truth to tell she didn't honestly know. It was enough just to get away.

Twenty minutes took care of the glassware, and after packing a few clothes into a suitcase Shelley went into the lounge.

'My dear, I wish I could say something to change your mind,' Janet said with genuine concern, but Shelley shook her head.

'Tell Mitch—that I'll write.'

Janet cast her an incredibly anxious look. 'Wait until he gets back,' she begged, then went on to warn, 'he's liable to be angry.'

'For a while, perhaps.' Shelley leant down and gave the older woman a quick hug, then almost ran from the house, down through the gardens to the garage.

Mitch had taken the sedan, which left her the choice of either the utility pick-up truck or the Range-Rover. There weren't all that many Range-Rovers around, and wishing to travel as inconspicuously as possible she elected to take the utility.

By the time Shelley had reached Mossman there

was a terrible feeling in the pit of her stomach that she should have heeded Janet's advice. But there was no turning back now.

A glance at her wristwatch showed it to be after six, and a momentary clutch of fear gripped her. It took an hour to drive to Cairns from Mossman, and an hour to drive back. Even allowing half an hour for Mitch to deposit Louise, Hal and Lynn at a motel, then drive Emma to the hospital, it would be impossible for her to avoid passing him on his way back. There was only one alternative—the road branching off to Port Douglas.

Without hesitating she took the turning when it came up some ten minutes later, and drove the three miles into the tiny township.

She chose a motel, rather than one of the two hotels, and booked in for one night, using the name Anderson. Ballantyne was too well known, and if Mitch sent out enquiries ...

The unit was small but neat, clean, and pleasantly furnished. There was a restaurant not far distant, but she didn't feel in the least like eating. However, common sense prevailed, and she walked down to the local dairy-cum-local-store where she bought some bread, a small tin of coffee, a few eggs and a jar of honey. If she became hungry later on she could have eggs on toast, followed by coffee. And if not— well, it would do nicely for breakfast in the morning. She bought a magazine to leaf through as well— at least with some reading matter and the television she should be able to pass the evening away until it was time to slip into bed.

As she walked past the motel office the manageress hurried out to ask if everything was in order, and Shelley hastily assured her that it was.

Inside the unit she looked idly around, experiencing a momentary sense of mad panic. What on earth was she doing here? Running away never solved anything, but the thought of confronting Mitch after the horrible things Emma had said took more courage than she possessed right now. Besides, there was an essence of logic behind those hateful words. It was possible, just barely possible, that Luke *had* cajoled Mitch into marriage.

The sooner she could get back to Brisbane, the flat, her pupils, the better. Perhaps she should check out of the motel in another hour when Mitch would have passed the Port Douglas turn-off, and drive on down to Cairns and catch the morning flight. Then she remembered that Louise, Hal and Lynn were in Cairns, and that they would be on that same flight tomorrow. Damn—that was that idea quashed! There was nothing else for it but to stay put until morning.

Half an hour of gazing into space didn't produce any further solution, and Shelley restlessly rose to her feet and went to the kitchen alcove to make some coffee, switching on the television set as she walked past it.

By the time the kettle had boiled the noise from the set was jarring on her nerves, like ragged steel on silk, and she hurriedly switched it off. Sitting down in an armchair, she began leafing through the magazine as she sipped her coffee, not really seeing anything on the pages as she flipped them over.

It was still light outside, and likely to remain so for another half hour. A walk along the beach might bring some order to her chaotic thoughts, she decided broodingly. Certainly she couldn't just *sit* here waiting for night to fall, to be followed, she hoped, by the merciful oblivion of sleep.

With undue haste she exchanged her skirt and jacket for a sundress, collected a cardigan and flung around her shoulders as she left the unit.

There was a slight breeze coming off the sea as she walked briskly along the road down on to the fringe of sand. It was soft and gritty, and after several yards she paused to slip off her sandals.

The tide was well on the turn, with perhaps another two hours before it lapped the foreshore, and nearby a few children were playing in the crisp white sand, their parents watching indulgently as a sandcastle took shape and became decorated with shells. Further along a group of teenagers were enjoying a boisterous game of handball, and Shelley envied them their carefree high spirits.

After a while she began wandering out towards the incoming tide, her eyes cast down as she searched idly for shells. The sand was hard and firm beneath her bare feet, and every now and then she paused to bend down and examine a shell that caught her attention. The fresh sea air smelt good, so clean. Soon she would turn and walk back, for the sun was low on the horizon and dusk came swiftly at this time of year, like the slow pulling down of a blind.

The teenagers had finished their game and were starting a fire for a barbecue when she walked past, and further on she saw that the children with their parents had already left. She paused to admire the sandcastle, then stooped to add the few shells she had collected.

As she straightened she had the uncanny sensation that someone was watching her actions, and she glanced casually back to glimpse a few couples strolling arm-in-arm a short distance away. They seemed immersed in their own world, and it was doubtful a lone girl would command their attention.

Once past the camping grounds Shelley made her way on to softer sand and glanced briefly ahead to check the distance to the road. Her footsteps faltered and came to a halt as she recognised that tall powerful frame silhouetted against the backdrop of rock.

For one crazy moment she wanted to turn and run, but her feet seemed rooted to the sand and refused to heed her brain.

He began strolling towards her with apparent ease, and as he drew close she felt the colour drain from her face. Halting less than a foot away, he stood regarding her in silence, his eyes dark and unfathomable. Both hands were thrust into his trouser pockets, and his shirt was left casually unbuttoned almost to the waist. There was an air of latent anger beneath the surface of his control that couldn't be ignored, in spite of his inscrutable expression.

'What are you doing here?' Shelley asked, so quietly that it came out as little more than a shaky whisper.

There was no change in his expression, and for the life of her she couldn't tear her eyes away from those dark tawny depths.

'That should be my query, don't you think?' Mitch alleged with silky detachment.

Her stomach began to curl painfully as she ran the edge of her tongue along her lower lip, and she nervously lifted a hand to push a stray lock of hair back behind one ear. He didn't intend making it easy for her, she could see. To parry words with him now would be akin to dicing with dynamite.

'I—needed to be alone for a while,' she managed

at last, and the eyes that had been regarding her raked her pale features ruthlessly.

'You intend coming back?'

There seemed nothing coherent she could say, and after timeless seconds she slowly shook her head. 'How did you know where to find me?' Was that her voice, so low and desolate?

'It was a calculated guess,' he answered dryly.

Shelley let her eyes slide down past that sensuously-moulded mouth to rest momentarily at the expanse of chest with its mat of curling hair visible in the deep vee between the front edges of his shirt. Her teeth began to worry the edge of her lip in a gesture of pure nervousness as she sought control of her rapid heartbeat.

'Correct, fortunately.' His voice was a slow sardonic drawl, and her eyes flew up to meet his. 'There are considerably more hotels and motels in Cairns,' he revealed wryly, 'in which to search out a runaway wife.'

Shelley felt the telltale rush of colour flood her cheeks and she swung abruptly away from him to gaze unseeing out over the sea to the distant horizon.

'I almost checked out an hour ago,' she offered unsteadily, and attempted to clear her throat of the sudden lump that rose to affect her voice. 'The thought of sharing the same flight as Louise ...' she trailed off shakily.

'Would have taken some explaining,' Mitch deduced with intended irony.

'Yes.'

There was a lengthy silence, and her eyes filled treacherously as her mind winged back over the happy years spent in the sprawling mansion she had come to regard as home. And her mother, and Luke.

With Mitch as the be-all and end-all in her young life.

'What are you doing?' came her startled query minutes later as his hand reached out and grasped her arm.

'What I'd like to do,' he hinted dryly, 'is render a thorough spanking. However, it's doubtful that would achieve anything.' He gave a faint sigh of exasperation and swung her round to face him. 'Dinner—I haven't eaten, and I don't imagine you have.'

'I'm not——'

'Don't argue, Shelley,' he commanded brusquely, his hold tightening measurably as he turned and began walking back along the sand to the road.

He paused when they reached the bitumen so that she could slip on her sandals, and her slightly incoherent,

'I won't be able to eat anything,' was met with a dark impenetrable look.

As they neared the restaurant she cast a nervous hand over the length of her hair, feeling its windblown dishevelment, and was swung off balance by his sudden perceptive glance.

'Leave it—you look fine.'

'I'm not in the least hungry,' she professed, only to have her protest ignored, and there was little else she could do other than accompany him inside.

She felt strangely enervated and incapable of struggling. In his present mood the consequences of resorting to such measures would doubtless prove unpleasant.

'A pleasure to see you here again, Mr Ballantyne,' the hostess bestowed charmingly, and Mitch accorded her an acknowledging nod before indicating with admirable geniality a table on the far side of the room.

'That table is eminently suitable—if it's not reserved?'

'Of course. If you would care to follow me?' She began to weave her way graciously between the tables, and Shelley had perforce to follow Mitch's broad back. The steel-like grip he had of her hand scarcely gave her much choice.

As soon as they were seated he scanned the menu with apparent ease, then ordered for them both, and Shelley began to wonder how she could possibly get through it all.

As it was a Friday evening the restaurant was well-patronised and there were not many empty tables. She let her gaze wander idly around the room, noting the exotic decor with interest. It hadn't changed at all since the last time she was here, almost two years ago, with Luke, Mitch, Janet and Ken to celebrate a birthday—was it hers, or——

'Yours,' Mitch told her dryly, and she swung startled smoky-blue eyes round to meet his sardonic expression.

'Reading my mind again?' she queried unsteadily.

He smiled lightly but didn't answer, and it was something of a relief when a waitress appeared with their first course.

The seafood cocktail was delectable, and Shelley could well have been content with that and missed the main course entirely, but her rather tentative manipulation of the contents of her plate—deliciously-presented barramundi fillets surrounded by an exotic array of salad greens—resulted in a decidely formidable frown being cast across the table.

'I really can't,' she stated hesitantly some ten minutes later when all she had managed to eat was a few mouthfuls of fish and even fewer of salad.

'Then leave it,' Mitch directed as he signalled the waitress to remove their plates, declining dessert and ordering coffee before sitting back in his chair to withdraw cigarettes and a lighter from his shirt pocket.

The coffee when it came was black and aromatic, and Shelley greeted its arrival with extreme relief. The silence between them was assuming cataclysmic proportions, and each time she thought of something to say it seemed so trivial as not to warrant mentioning.

'Our—honeymoon, for want of a better word,' Mitch began in a slow gravelly drawl that sounded like granulated honey, 'hasn't exactly had a propitious beginning.'

Shelley looked at him, then looked hastily down at her coffee. She was such a mass of jangling nerves it wasn't funny, and it simply wasn't fair that he should sit there and play cat to her mouse.

'The whole thing was contrived to please Luke,' she ventured slowly.

'Which it did. He died a happy man.'

There seemed nothing to add to that, and she carefully picked up her cup in both hands to sip the contents with concentrated dedication.

'Finished?'

She replaced her empty cup with hands that weren't quite steady and nodded silently, following suit as Mitch stood easily to his feet. She walked ahead of him and wandered on outside as he paused to settle the bill.

It was pleasantly cool in the clear night air, and

there were lights glimmering in the darkness. Shelley sensed him behind her and half-turned, risking a quick glance up at that rugged profile, searching for some sign of what he intended next.

'The motel, I think,' he announced obliquely, and she had little option but to walk beside him—several hundred yards that grew less and less, with the butterflies inside her stomach fighting for room, screaming to get out.

'Inside, Shelley.' Curt words that brooked no argument as he held open the door, and she stepped into the lounge before turning slowly round to face him.

'I was going to write,' she began apprehensively, meeting that clear amber gaze.

'An explanation?' His query was silk-smooth and dangerous, and she shivered involuntarily.

'Yes.'

He seemed to take a long time before passing comment, although his eyes never left hers for a second. 'I'll save you the trouble,' he drawled softly. 'Tell me now.'

Shelley took a deep breath and hugged her arms together across her bosom, feeling suddenly cold. 'I wanted to make it easy for you,' she managed with remarkable steadiness.

One eyebrow quirked in silent sardonic query.

'It seemed best. No—embarrassing confrontation ...' she trailed off distantly.

'I thought I was well versed in the contrariness of the female mind,' Mitch drawled with wry cynicism. 'But with you, everything becomes a whole new ball-game.' He looked down at her hard and long. 'Tell me, what were you going to do when you arrived in Brisbane? Go back to the flat—each school?'

When she didn't answer he took a step closer and took her chin between finger and thumb and tilted it.

'Our marriage vows—what did you expect to do about them?' he queried softly.

Her lips began to tremble disastrously and she ran her tongue along the lower edge in an attempt to effect some semblance of control.

'It shouldn't be difficult to arrange an annulment.' Strange that she should sound so calm when a pulse throbbed rapidly at her temple and her breathing was anything but steady. There was a note of anguish in her voice as she rushed on heedlessly. 'You'll want to get married—really married.'

'I am married,' he drawled slowly. 'To you.'

She had absolutely no hope of preventing the tears from welling up behind her eyes. 'Don't—stop this game you're pl-playing with me—please,' she begged tremulously.

'Stop?' he queried with quiet emphasis. 'I wasn't aware I'd begun.'

'It should have never got as far as marriage,' she reflected shakily, blinking hard against threatening tears. 'Luke would have been just as happy with an engagement—it isn't so difficult to discard.'

'What makes you think I might want to?' he questioned smoothly, his eyes darkening as he witnessed one solitary tear spill over and roll slowly down her cheek.

'Why shouldn't you?' she countered miserably.

'Emma,' Mitch shrugged dryly, and smiled a little as she gave an incredulous gasp. 'Ken, Janet—they each had some interesting observations to make, repeating a conversation or two they'd managed to overhear.'

Her eyes shimmered with unshed tears at the vivid recollection of Emma's spiteful words.

'Perhaps you'd better see this,' he continued significantly as he withdrew a folded sheet of paper and opened it out before handing it to her.

With shaking fingers Shelley took it and tried to focus on the typescript. It was a legal deed of some kind, and the signature at the bottom of the page was his own. She began to read, discovering to her consternation that he had gifted her an amount equal to that of Luke's bequest.

'Look at the date, Shelley,' Mitch bade quietly, and her eyes widened measurably.

Twelve days ago! That was——

'The day I collected you from Brisbane,' he delared steadily. 'Does that disprove the theoretical carrot supposedly dangled in front of my nose?'

She lifted shaky fingers to brush away the solitary tear resting at the edge of her chin, then gazed up at him wordlessly.

'My wedding gift to you,' he revealed gently.

'I haven't anything,' she faltered remorsefully timeless seconds later.

'You have,' he divulged steadily. 'Yourself—something I consider beyond price.'

Now the tears did fall, slowly, one after the other.

'As to the rest of it ... Not even for Luke would I permit myself to be manoeuvred into a marriage of convenience.'

'Why didn't you tell me?' she beseeched achingly.

'Reflect a little,' he said quietly, watching intently as a puzzled frown momentarily creased her brow.

'I didn't think you meant *me*,' she explained slowly after a considerable length of time, and glimpsed his wry smile.

'My darling goose, how could you *not* know?' He lowered his head and gently caressed her brow with his lips, letting them rove slowly down to her mouth, and there was a wealth of seduction in his touch.

'If I'd followed my baser instincts,' he enlightened softly, 'you would have become a child-bride at seventeen. But you had the right to a few carefree years in which to grow and find yourself before being committed into one man's care for a lifetime.' He paused fractionally and a whimsical smile widened his lips. 'I had to make do with a brotherly kiss at vacation time or during any one of my infrequent trips down to Brisbane.'

'Brotherly?' Shelley expostulated wonderingly, remembering each and every one of those occasions with remarkable clarity.

'Yours wasn't exactly a sisterly response,' Mitch reminded tolerantly, and there was a wicked gleam in those amber depths as he witnessed her confusion.

'I didn't seem to be able to help myself,' she explained slowly. 'You've been my whole world for almost as long as I can remember. Wherever I was, you were there in my thoughts, filling my dreams. Yours was the face I saw, the lips I wished for every moment I was away.'

The warmth in his eyes proved her undoing, and one tear spilled and ran slowly down her cheek.

'If you look at me like that for long, I think I'll——' she began tremulously as he drew her close against him, and those last few words became lost as his mouth descended on hers.

'What do you say to a few days on Green Island?' he suggested musingly endless minutes later. 'We could catch the launch from Cairns in the morning.'

Shelley gave him a singularly sweet smile as she

reached up and wound her arms around his neck. 'Couldn't we stay here? It doesn't matter where, does it?'

'Not in the least,' Mitch answered gently, kissing her with a sensual expertise that engulfed her in an emotional tide so tumultuous it almost made her cry out when he raised his head.

'Dear Shelley,' he murmured softly, his eyes alert and sensually alive as he gazed down at her. 'I love you—so much so, I doubt I could exist without you.'

Her heart took wings, soaring heavenward as she smiled witchingly up at him. 'You won't have to, Mitchell Ballantyne,' she assured him enchantingly.

'Have you forgotten *your* name is now Ballantyne?' he queried quizzically, and she grinned, unabashed.

'I was wondering when you'd remember that.' Gently teasing words that caused him to plant a brief hard kiss on her mouth.

'Minx,' he mocked gently.

Shelley laughed as she hid sparkling eyes from his frankly sensuous gaze, only to have him tilt her chin, and at the unasked question in those dark tawny depths she quickly sobered.

There was a sensation of time standing still, then slowly of their own volition her fingers lifted to caress his lips, and her eyes widened into large smoky-blue pools as he caught her hand and turned his mouth into her palm.

'I love you,' she said unsteadily. 'I can't honestly remember a time when I haven't.'

His arms gathered her close as his mouth ravished hers with an ardent savagery that cast aside any vestige of doubt, and she became treacherously lost in the expertise of his touch.

Without a word he swung her up into his arms and moved towards the bedroom, and his hands were gentle as he lowered her down to stand in front of him.

'You see how it is with me?' Deep, huskily spoken words that belied control, and the fingers that traced the outline of her lips were not quite steady.

'Does that mean you intend keeping me under close surveillance for a while?' Shelley teased bewitchingly, revelling in the warmth of his smile.

'You'd better believe for the rest of my life,' Mitch vowed softly.

Without a word she placed a hand each side of his face and drew it down to hers, sure in the knowledge that he was her reason for living—that together they belonged, almost as if fate itself had decreed it.

# Take your holiday romance with you.

STARFIRE – Celia Scott.
CHANCE MEETINGS – Vanessa James.
SAVAGE PAGAN – Helen Bianchin.
HARD TO GET – Carole Mortimer.

Price £4.40

**Mills & Boon**
THE ROSE OF ROMANCE